SILENT CRAVINGS

ELITE HEIRS OF MANHATTAN
BOOK 4

MISSY WALKER

Cover Design: Missy Walker

Editor: Swish Design & Editing

To all the mommas x

CONTENT NOTES

This story contains sensitive themes related to pregnancy loss that may be difficult for some readers.

Elite *Men* Of Manhattan and
Elite *Heirs* of Manhattan Family Tree

BARRETT BLACK LOURDE DIAMOND	CONNOR DIAMOND PEPPER LITTLE	ARI GOLDSMITH OLIVIA WILLOWS	MAGNUS MILLER EVELYN BLACK
FORBIDDEN LUST #1 **FORBIDDEN LOVE #2**	**LOST LOVE #3**	**MISSING LOVE #4**	**GUARDED LOVE #5**

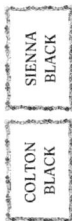

COLTON BLACK	SIENNA BLACK	LUCIAN DIAMOND	ROSE GOLDSMITH	NOAH GOLDSMITH	ARIA MILLER	VALENTINA MILLER	MILES YOUNG

SEDUCTIVE HEARTS #1 COLTON AND ROSE	SWEET SURRENDER #2 NOAH AND SIENNA	SINFUL DESIRES #3 ARIA AND MILES	SILENT CRAVINGS #4 VALENTINA AND EVAN

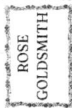

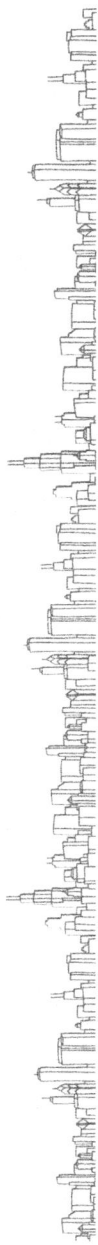

1

VALENTINA

Rose was pregnant.

We thought this was an engagement party, but my cousin, Colton, went and added the fact they were having a baby.

I wasn't prepared for this. Just like I wasn't prepared to hear the news with dozens of people around me. Especially not someone who hadn't stopped watching me no matter how I silently wished he would find something, *anything* else to look at.

Everyone was clapping, giving hugs, and squealing with excitement. Some were already bombarding Rose with questions about baby showers and such. Yet, all I could do was grip the stem of my champagne flute a little tighter and hope with literally every part of me that no one expected my enthusiasm.

I didn't want to come off as a petty bitch who couldn't handle her friends' happiness. Besides, Colton was my cousin. This was about more than friendship alone. They were going to expand our family. But no matter how much I tried, I was frozen to my spot, a wave of anxiety rolling through me.

The announcement felt like a complete kick in the stomach.

"Shit, I didn't expect them to start popping out kids for a while yet." As usual, Lucian found an eloquent way to express himself. He looked at me, then at Evan, and was clearly let down by our lack of a reaction. "Fine," he mumbled, draining his glass. "Guess I'll go congratulate them or something."

He didn't know—at least, I didn't think he did. Nobody had ever mentioned us in the years since our fling fizzled out, so I had always assumed Evan was just as tight-lipped about it as I had been. Only my twin sister knew, and even then, I wouldn't have told her if I thought it was something I could've hidden from her. One of the downfalls of having a twin, I guess.

I scanned the room, seeking her out, finding her standing with an arm around Miles' waist as they waited their turn to congratulate the parents-to-be. Twins had a funny way of understanding each other. It was like she felt me watching her, though she only offered a bright smile and tried to wave me over. When I stood still, her smile slipped away, and worry lines etched themselves across her brow.

All those years ago, lying on the bathroom floor.

Weak.

Dizzy.

Trying to pretend as if it had never happened. Then mustering the strength to ask my sister one thing while she witnessed me at my worst.

"Promise me, Aria. Promise me never to mention this ever again. I want to forget this. No, I need to forget this."

"But, Val..."

"No!" My frail voice reverberated throughout the bathroom as she looked down at me and whispered,

"I promise."

Now she got it.

We were on the same page.

And I kind of hated her for it because we were never ever supposed to talk about that awful night.

If I went on as if it had never happened, then it couldn't be true—out of sight, out of mind, and all that. This eighteen-year-old logic had worked well for me over the last decade. Besides, it wasn't something I could afford to dwell on. If I did, it might consume me.

I downed what was left of my champagne before deciding to go for something a little stronger and less sugary. I didn't need a killer hangover in the morning. With the bar in Rose's kitchen pretty much less crowded now that everybody was gathered around the happy couple, I could fix myself a proper dirty martini, which I downed before pouring another. Why not? I wasn't driving.

"Can you believe it?" Sienna was practically bouncing on the balls of her feet when she found me drinking alone. "That is going to be one beautiful child. I can't believe the idiot didn't say anything," she added, referring to her brother, Colton.

"I guess they wanted it to be a surprise," I pointed out with a shrug. "Anyway, we all know now."

"No wonder they went to dinner with the parents earlier instead of inviting them here," she mused, gathering a few empty bottles and rinsing them in the sink. "I guess they must have broken the news then to make it more special."

"I'm sure it was special," I agreed, torn between nursing the martini and chugging it. There wasn't enough vodka in the bottle to soothe the throbbing ache in my chest or the sarcasm on the tip of my tongue. "I mean, breaking the news in front of a bunch of strangers at a restaurant?"

"You sound like somebody pissed in your martini glass." She was still laughing joyfully when she made this observation, totally oblivious, probably a little tipsy and over the moon at the idea of being an aunt.

For the first time in ten years, I wished I hadn't kept things a secret. Maybe then she would understand the gut punch of being reminded all at once of what could have been. Then again, what difference would it make? I'd have everybody feeling weird and awkward around me when it came time for announcements like this. I didn't want that either. I wasn't anybody's object to pity. Anything but that.

"It's a little loud in here," I mumbled, sipping slowly since I was no longer alone in the room. "Just a headache. That's all."

She looked like she didn't believe me but knew better than to press me on it. I wasn't exactly what anybody would call patient on a good day, and this was not shaping up to be the best.

What would it have been like being a mom all these years?

That was a stupid question, completely impossible to answer. I gritted my teeth against it and bolted back what was left in my glass when Sienna wasn't looking. I wouldn't be able to get away without congratulating them, so I returned to the living room and made a point to smile and be happy while waiting to talk to the happy couple.

"You are just the person I wanted to talk to," Rose told me after a hug so tight I was glad to escape with my ribs intact. "This is really going to mess with the wedding planning. I don't want to be super far along."

"We don't have to think about that right now," I told her since there was only so much I could handle all at once.

"But still," she insisted. "It's really going to push things up. Are you going to be okay with that?"

"Sweetie." I took her face in my hands. "It is so like you to worry about everybody else except yourself at a time like this. But I am telling you, everything's going to be great." That was what I did. I told people things they needed to believe while I took the brunt of the weight of figuring things out. I'd sort of made a career out of it.

"Yeah, don't insult her." Colton winked at me. "She's the most organized, kick-ass person I know. She can make miracles happen. Can't you, Valentina?"

"Butter me up all you want, cousin," I told him. "I'm still charging for my services."

At least that got Rose laughing instead of being so anxious. "I just don't want anybody to be put out too much. Though I still want everything to be perfect," she added.

"It will be. Didn't your baby daddy just say so?" If I could make jokes, that meant I'd be all right. Didn't it? It was just a surprise, that's all. Nothing more than that. I could handle this. After all, I had handled it all these years, carrying a secret I couldn't imagine sharing with anybody but my sister, Aria. But then, that was only because I didn't have a choice.

I was a grown woman with experience under her belt. My own business, a phone full of contacts representing an enormous network of clients and associates. I had my shit together.

Life turned out the way it was meant to.

Somehow, I couldn't quite swallow the thought as truth. Nor did it stop me from craving another drink with my entire being. Anything to ease the persistent ache in my chest.

I promised Rose I would visit her office on Monday

morning so we could go over a revised timeline for the wedding. If anything, it would give me something to focus on that didn't involve my fucked-up past poor decision-making.

Where the hell was Evan?

I didn't want to see him. Something told me I wouldn't be able to hold it together if I did. With any luck, he would be in the process of working his way into some dumb girl's panties by now.

Usually, a thought like that would make me snicker to myself. Like most men, he was ruled by his dick. Add looks and money, and you'd end up with a recipe for a guy who could get laid just about anywhere any time. I'd normally laugh off the constant search for pussy. At most, I'd roll my eyes and make jokes about buying stock in a condom company. Now, though, the idea of him moving on with his night without a second thought left me thirstier than ever.

I returned to the kitchen and refilled my glass, ignoring the excited and semidrunken chatter around me. When was the last time I had tried to numb myself like this? I couldn't afford to think of it that way, not in front of so many people. This was self-preservation, pure and simple.

"Whoa, there." I didn't notice Noah coming up behind me until I stumbled while turning away from the bar. He caught me laughing softly. "Maybe you need to slow down a little," he suggested.

Maybe you need to mind your own business. Right, because that wouldn't look completely out of line and out of nowhere. "I'm good," I assured him, and I even managed to give him a little smile. "Really. I'm fine."

The idiot insisted on leaning back and waving a hand in front of his face. "You smell like you just took a bath in a bottle of Smirnoff," he informed me. "How many of me do you see right now?"

"Fuck off." I ended with a laugh, and he joined me, but those lines between his eyebrows didn't shift even a tiny bit. If anything, they got deeper. No matter what he thought, I wasn't so drunk I couldn't see straight.

"Sienna said you have a headache," he explained because suddenly everyone was obsessed with me. "Maybe this isn't where you need to be right now."

"Since when are you my nanny?" I grumbled. His head snapped back a little. I'd gone too far. "Sorry," I offered, trying to cover for my attitude. "I guess I have had too much. Maybe I should go home so I don't ruin anything."

"Nobody said you were ruining anything." He reached out to awkwardly pat my shoulder. "It happens. Remember the night I drank all that tequila and wound up face down in the middle of your living room? Who helped me clean myself up?"

"That was sort of selfish on my part," I reminded him as I flinched at the memory. "I didn't want my first apartment stinking like puke."

"The point stands." With a grin, he asked, "Do you want me to get you home? Make sure you get in okay?"

I was tipsy. I wasn't fall-down drunk. "No, it's cool. I'll get an Uber or something."

He wasn't listening, too busy lifting a hand to get Evan's attention. "Hey! Evan!"

"Not necessary," I warned, though it was too late.

Dammit, I should have left before now.

It's not like anybody would have missed me except maybe Aria, but then she was busy canoodling with our stepbrother and boyfriend, so she probably wouldn't notice I was gone.

Shit, I had drank too much. Whenever I started getting depressed and dark, that was my red flag.

Evan had heard him and was now coming our way, weaving in and out of clusters of guests. Why did he have to look so good?

When we were kids, he was cute, even hot. Soulful dark eyes, a jaw so sharp it could etch glass, not to mention the way he was blessed with a naturally tall, slim body that put him half a head taller than most people in any room he entered. In other words, he garnered attention. My attention, to be exact.

Ten years had taken him from a cute kid to an incredibly sexy, intriguing man. Sure, he could be a pain in the ass with his irreverent sense of humor and the fact he sometimes forgot how to censor himself, but I knew where that came from. I knew him better than our friends thought I did.

"You don't look so good," he told me, looking me up and down while running a hand through the wild, dark hair he always wore just long enough to curl around his earlobes and the nape of his neck. "Are you feeling all right?"

He was trying too hard to pretend he didn't know what I was going through. If it hadn't been for the look we exchanged right after the announcement, I might have believed him. I mean, he had no trouble moving on after us. After what happened. I doubted there was a single day he looked back on the time and wondered what life would look like today if things had turned out differently.

"Can you see her home?" Noah asked as if I wasn't standing right next to him.

"It's fine. I'll get an Uber," I insisted.

It was better to ignore Evan. I had worked so damn hard to put everything behind me, to forget. Now, here I was with everything thrown in my face all over again. I couldn't look at him. It was too hard.

"I can at least ride with you," he offered. "There isn't much of anything interesting going on here anyway." He looked around, smirking. I didn't have to ask what he meant by that. A party always led to him getting his dick wet.

"Wouldn't want to stick around to support your friends," I muttered. I would have guessed he didn't hear me, but the clench of a muscle in his jaw told me otherwise.

"Great. Thanks." Noah gave my shoulder another awkward pat. It was obvious he was proud of himself for taking care of me. Such a hero.

None of this was his fault. I had to remind myself of that as I ducked into Rose's bedroom closet after fighting my way through the guests. Being a lifelong friend offered certain privileges, and I took advantage of the brief moment of quiet, breathing slowly and letting my muscles loosen. I considered leaving a note on the nightstand to explain why I left early but decided against it. What was I supposed to say anyway? *It's too damn hard to be here right now, so I'm running away.* Sure, that would work. I rolled my eyes at myself on my way out of the room, heading straight for the front door in hopes of escaping before Evan could find me. Of all people to be holed up in a car next to, he was the furthest down on my list.

Luck was not in my favor. There he was, waiting for me, offering a tight little grin before opening the front door and ushering me through. Well, this didn't have to be terrible. It was only a ten-minute ride to my apartment in Hudson Yards. We didn't even have to speak.

I should've known better.

"Did you have dinner tonight?" he asked, seemingly out of nowhere, on the way down to the lobby. The air in the elevator car felt too thick, too challenging to pull into my lungs. And he wanted me to think about when I last ate?

"I had a salad," I told him after thinking about it.

"When?"

"I don't know. Three, maybe? I had a busy day."

"That's a late lunch. Not dinner," he grumbled. "No wonder the booze hit you so hard."

"Thank you, Captain Obvious," I whispered once the doors opened to the lobby. It was a relief to get out of the elevator and put a little space between us while checking the app to see if the car was getting closer. "The driver's just rounding the corner now," I told him, glad for the excuse to hurry out of the building. The cool, wet air hit my face once I reached the sidewalk, remnants of the day's rain. The light mist offered me a moment to breathe, a complete contrast to the suffocating warmth shared in the elevator.

He opened the door for me when the Range Rover pulled up in front of the building but said nothing until we were on our way. "It's early," he offered. "We could stop off someplace, grab something to eat. I'm starved."

Why couldn't he leave me alone? That was all I wanted, more than anything in the world. To be alone. To let the mask drop, crawl into bed, and maybe spend all of Sunday there wallowing.

When I didn't say anything because I didn't trust myself to, he continued, "Is that Chinese place on the corner still good? I remember I loved their orange chicken."

My molars ground hard before I grunted. "Yeah, they're good."

"I'll place an order now." He was already on the phone, opening an app and adding items to a cart. "What would you like?"

For you to shut the fuck up and leave me be.

I would have liked him to stop trying to insert himself into my life. I would have liked to ask him why the fuck he cared so much all of a sudden when ten years ago, he didn't give a damn.

I didn't trust myself to permanently ruin our relationship, so I settled for, "Dumplings and an eggroll would be good. And wonton soup," I added, imagining the shape I'd be in tomorrow. Soup would be easy to heat up.

"Got it." His knee bounced up and down as he gazed out the window to his left. We were crawling down 34th Street, moving so slowly we may as well not have moved at all. I could've walked home faster than this.

Why the hell was nothing going in my favor tonight?

When the spicy, familiar scent of his cologne hit me all at once, tears sprang to my eyes. He was still wearing it. Not always, since this was the first time in a long time I recognized the scent.

Of all nights, he would have to wear it now.

I could still remember being wrapped in his sweatshirt, the scent all around me as I sat on the foot of his bed.

"Are you sure?" He hadn't closed his mouth since it fell open when I gave him the news. I wasn't sure he had taken a breath like he turned into a statue before those three words tumbled past his lips.

"I took three tests. They say you have to wait a few minutes, but the lines showed up, like, instantly." I ran my hand under my eyes to catch fresh tears.

How did I have any moisture left in me after crying my eyes out in the hours since I took those tests? Wondering what I was supposed to do. Whether he would hate me or think I tried to trap him by getting pregnant.

He crossed the room slowly, then sat down next to me, putting a hand on my leg but not saying anything for a long time.

I wanted to give him a minute to get himself together, but at the same time, I would die if I didn't know what he was thinking. "Are you okay?" I finally whispered. "I'm so sorry. I didn't mean for this to happen. I thought we were being safe."

"Me too." He scrubbed his other hand over his face before running his fingers through his thick, black hair. Eyeing the suitcases in the far corner, waiting to be taken to Harvard, he muttered, "Shit. We're not ready for this."

"I know," I sniffled. "I get it."

"I mean, we literally can't handle it," he insisted.

"I hear you." I also heard what sounded like anger creeping into his voice. "You don't have to tell me that. There is nothing you could say that I haven't told myself already today."

"Does anybody know besides me?"

"Only the woman who was at the register when I bought the tests."

"Magnus would fucking kill me if he ever found out."

And that was when I knew. He had no intention of ever telling anybody about us, about the baby, any of it. What did I expect? For him to suddenly have a change of heart? Realize how much he really cared about me, that we were more than just a fling one summer between high school and college? Ice pierced my veins before I brushed his hand off my leg.

All of a sudden, the thought of being touched by him was repulsive. "Don't worry," I told him, getting up. "Dad never has to know. Nobody has to know. Your life won't change in any way."

"Wait. Don't start that shit with me."

It was like he deliberately wanted to find the worst thing to say. Like I needed him to have an attitude with me on maybe the most emotional day of my life.

"Here." I pulled off his sweatshirt and tossed it on the bed, straightening out the T-shirt I wore underneath. "I don't want to

inconvenience you." He muttered something halfhearted, but that was it. No getting up, no hugging me, or asking what I needed.

How could I have been so wrong about him?

I ignored his weak-ass attempts at stopping me from leaving his room and his life. Not that it was possible to ever really be out of each other's lives, with him being best friends with my cousin, but we would never get back what we lost.

"We're here." His sudden announcement yanked me out of my haze of memories and into the present, where we sat double-parked in front of the brightly lit takeout joint.

Now, there was nothing for me to do but go along with him since I knew he wouldn't stop until he got his way. Time might have changed a lot of things, but it hadn't changed that.

I just had to go through the motions of getting this over with so I could be alone with my pain.

2

EVAN

You would think those skyscraper heels of hers would make her walk slower. Instead, I had to practically run to keep up with Valentina as she left the Chinese place and crossed the street without looking back to make sure I was with her.

"Hold up!" I called out when it looked like she was entering her building without waiting for me to get through the door, which would lock automatically once it closed.

She was drunk, maybe not fall-down drunk, but just enough to slur her words. Otherwise, she didn't miss a step, crossing the tile lobby in a distractingly short skirt and jabbing a finger against the button to call the elevator. Her phone was in her other hand, and her thumb moved over the screen like lightning.

"What's so important this time on a Saturday night?" I asked, leaning in to check her screen. Really, I was trying to thaw the ice that had formed between us in the car. I had to do something to break through the wall she put around her.

She snatched the phone away from my view, holding it

close to her chest. A nice chest, a chest it took serious self-control not to stare at on a regular basis.

Tonight, there was a nice bit of cleavage showing thanks to a low-cut shirt. Me being so much taller than her didn't hurt either.

"None of your busi-nesss," she retorted with a little slur at the end, tossing her rich, brown waves over her shoulder before glaring at me with familiar, sapphire blue eyes. "You might have convinced me to eat with you, but that doesn't mean you get to read my messages."

"Excuse me. I didn't know you were exchanging secrets with somebody."

"If you must know, I'm typing out a list of things I need to do for the wedding. Rose said something about wanting to move it up so she's not too far along with the baby." She kept typing, staring down at the phone while her shiny pink nails moved over the screen.

The baby.

Say something, you dumb fuck. But what? That was the thing. The time to say something was ten years ago. Ever since then, every hour we'd spent together pushed us a little further apart. Like two boats drifting in opposite directions. By now, she was so far away she might have been a dot on the horizon.

Sorry, I totally fucked up when you told me about the baby? Sorry it scared the shit out of me, and I was too fucking young and stupid to know what to say? Hell, who was I kidding? If somebody came to me right now, this very minute, and told me they were pregnant with my kid, I would probably shit my pants. Kids were no more part of my life plan now than they were when I was eighteen and about to start college.

There were still no answers by the time we reached one of the building's upper floors. The doors opened to the dimly lit hallway of what used to be a warehouse but had been converted to loft apartments somewhere along the way.

As always, on entering the loft, I admired the exposed brick and the open, spacious feeling. The living room was two stories high with a metal staircase leading up to an open suite which, last I knew, Valentina used as her bedroom and home office. The first floor was composed of the living room plus an open kitchen, a small dining area with a powder room beyond it, and a corner of the floor devoted to a reading nook.

It was one thing I always liked about her. She had her wild days when we were kids, and she busted her ass building a business out of nothing, but in her downtime, she liked to curl up in an overstuffed chair and read while surrounded by houseplants. I couldn't remember the last time I met a woman who could talk about books. The latest social media trends, sure, but not books.

"I think I'm going to go up and get changed." She kicked off her heels, knocking a few inches off her still-tall frame. She left them where they landed and waved a hand as she climbed the stairs. "Just put the food out wherever. Help yourself to a drink if you want."

Not exactly five-star hospitality, but I didn't expect it. It was enough just being with her again.

The breakfast bar separating the kitchen from the living room seemed like as good of a place as any to eat, so I arranged the containers on the quartz countertop before hunting in the kitchen for sriracha and soy sauce, forks, and water for Valentina. She would need it after downing those martinis.

She wasn't exactly being sneaky back there about gulping down anything she could get her hands on. At least, that was how it looked to me whenever I glanced her way, more often than I should have.

It hurt her earlier. She may as well have written the words on her forehead. And why not? Hell, I thought about her as soon as the word *baby* was mentioned. Thinking back, I couldn't remember exactly why. People had babies all the time. I couldn't walk down the street without side-stepping a stroller.

I had wanted to push Lucian out of the way and wrap my arms around her. Why? Maybe because she looked like somebody kicked her hard. Because it had been ten years since I saw her with the same pained strain across her beautiful face.

And, of course, I was the asshole who made her look that way the first time.

Maybe a drink wasn't a bad idea. At the party, I had taken it pretty easy, sticking to a couple of glasses of scotch. I found a bottle in the kitchen and poured a modest amount into a glass before adding cubes from the freezer.

Valentina had changed into soft cotton shorts and an oversized sweatshirt. Incredible the way changing clothes and hair could take years off a woman's age. Her feet were bare, her long, brown locks in a bun on top of her head by the time she padded down the stairs.

How the hell was she hotter this way than she was before? Softer, more real somehow. My mouth went dry, and I had to look away from her before she saw the yearning written across my face.

"Is this a hint?" She picked up the bottle of water I had left on the counter.

I could only handle so much sarcasm before my patience wore thin. "Yeah. Drink some damn water. Eat

some food." I shoved a paper-wrapped eggroll her way.
"Grease helps too."

"You'd think this was the first time I ever drank," she
muttered. "Besides, I didn't have all that much. I wasn't
feeling well, and it was an excuse to get out of there." She
peeled the wax paper away from the eggroll and took a bite
before adding a packet of duck sauce.

Why did she feel the need to lie? Like anybody with eyes
couldn't tell she'd been actively trying to get wasted, which
wasn't like her.

"It was pretty crowded in there," I offered. What the fuck
was wrong with me? I had known this girl since I first met
Colton and Noah in high school. Almost fifteen years. Yet I
couldn't get my brain and my mouth working together. Not
tonight.

It was crazy how a happy announcement could unlock a
door that had been closed for a decade. "You know me.
Crowded spaces aren't a problem. They're sort of my bread
and butter." Slapping a palm to her forehead, she pulled her
phone from her sweatshirt pocket and typed furiously.

"What is it this time?" I asked, spearing a piece of spicy
chicken.

"I need to make finding the venue my number one priority," she muttered while typing. "This is going to be a real
bitch."

Offer up one of the country clubs, you idiot. But that would
mean working side by side through this, and if tonight were
anything to go by, that would be the last thing she'd want.

"You'll make it work," I predicted around a mouthful of
fried rice, deciding it for the best to keep quiet. "You always
do." I wasn't all that hungry, but the food was as good as I'd
remembered.

Instinct told me not to leave her alone tonight. Not until

she went to bed anyway. It was the least I could do after fucking up spectacularly back in the day.

"I guess it's for the best." I held the phone close to my ear, turning my back on the guys as we waited in line for breakfast in the dining hall three weeks into my first semester. "I mean, this wasn't the right time for either of us, you know?"

Stupid asshole. *She was so quiet for so long I thought she'd hung up. No, the call was still active, which meant she was there. She just didn't want to speak to me.*

"Right?" I prompted.

"Yeah. You're right." She sounded like a ghost—empty. How was a girl supposed to sound the morning after she had a miscarriage? "I'll let you go. You sound busy."

I should have left the fucking dining hall. I should have gotten in the car and driven out to her. I should've done a lot of things. But I was eighteen, stupid, and just found out I wasn't going to be a father.

The shitty thing was, I ate breakfast feeling better than I had in weeks, ever since Valentina told me about the baby the weekend before I was due to move to Cambridge.

I wouldn't know where to begin apologizing now. Would it be trite if I brought it up? It was the elephant in the room, that much was obvious. Or was I telling myself that? Was it guilt compelling me to torture myself this way?

"I don't know why I let you talk me into this." She pushed her food away after picking at it halfheartedly, still more interested in her phone. "I'm not really hungry."

"You just hate the idea of anyone trying to take care of you."

"Right..." she sighed, "... because you know me so well."

I did. I might not have shown it outwardly, but I paid attention. I always had. From the day we met when Colton introduced me to his friends and family at school, there was something about her that drew me in. "*I'm Valentina Miller, and anybody with the balls to be friends with my idiot cousin is worth knowing.*" That snarky, smirking first impression was all it took for her to fascinate me.

She went through the motions of packing up what was left while I continued picking at my chicken. She may as well have been miles away with layers of barbed wire wrapped around her. Everything about her body language told me to steer clear—the hunched shoulders, tight jaw, not to mention the way she refused to look at me when I tried to catch her eye.

"What's on your mind?" I asked when she finished cleaning up after herself.

I would've been safer lighting a match in a gas-filled room. She exploded in a flurry of waving hands which she then slammed onto the counter. "Why does anything have to be the matter, for fuck's sake? Jesus Christ."

"Jesus fuck, Valentina. Is it that time of the month or something?"

Her face bloomed red-bloody murder. "You're the one who insisted on coming here when I didn't want to be around people!"

"How was I supposed to know you didn't wanna be around people?"

"Because I told you I just wanted to go home, genius." She tapped the side of her head while giving me a dirty look before turning her back and facing the sink.

I could almost feel the heat coming off her, even with the countertop between us. Her shoulders rose and fell with each ragged breath she took. She was struggling. All I wanted was to reach out, but what good would it do? If I could find the words, what would I say that would change a damn thing? And how fucking empty would it sound after all these years?

When I thought about it, I realized I couldn't remember a single time my father had ever apologized for anything, and he'd had more than enough reason to. It was beneath him, and like me, he had not been raised to do it.

A pathetic excuse. I knew it in my bones as I got up from my stool and rounded the counter separating the two rooms. Was I taking my life in my hands, approaching a rabid animal who might bite? Maybe. But I knew a lot of this had to do with me. There was no way it didn't. The least I could do was try to offer what awkward comfort I could, no matter if I felt like an inept fuck approaching her from behind, laying gentle hands on her shoulders.

"You don't have to do that," she muttered, her head hanging low.

Was she sniffling?

"I'm..." *Sorry.* Just tell her you're fucking sorry. Something closed my throat, turning it into a pinhole. My tongue was thick and useless. I would only upset her more if I drudged it all up again. Maybe that was what I needed to believe.

"You're what?" She turned, glaring up at me with defiance flashing in her eyes. Energy crackled when they met mine like a hum of electricity that, for some reason, went straight to my dick and got it twitching. She was right here in front of me. I had never been able to resist her when she was like this. I didn't want to back away and give her space. The fire burning in her eyes wouldn't burn me.

And if it did... I would live with the scars.

"I'm here," I settled on replying. "I am right here. You don't have to be alone."

"What if that's what I want?" she whispered, softening

under my touch. I could feel the tension draining, the muscles loosening, her resistance fading. I stepped up closer, my body brushing hers.

"What if that's what you're telling yourself?" I countered. "You can lie to a lot of people, but you can't lie to me. You never could."

"There you go again, acting like you know me." She made a move to escape, shifting her weight like she was going to slide past me.

Not a fucking chance. I held her, growling, "Stop running, dammit."

"Did you ever wonder why I would want to run from you?" Her eyes were shining with unshed tears, her chin trembling.

I couldn't answer. I could only take her face in my hands the way I had so many times before. She was warm and familiar. And *here,* intoxicating me the way she always had. In all these damn years, she'd never been this close.

She scoffed when I didn't answer her right away and tried to get past me again. This time, I did what instinct demanded. I leaned down to claim her soft, sweet lips.

A jolt ran through her like a current passing through her body. I knew the feeling since the first touch of her lips to mine was a rush, unlike anything I had felt in a decade. Something about her did something to me no other woman ever had. Now, that translated into a rush of searing heat surging through me that had my dick hardening and left me wondering how I had spent years without doing this without tasting or touching her.

You had to forget her.

Once the wave of surprise passed, she touched her hands to my chest. Instead of pushing me away, though, she twisted my shirt in her clenched fists. The soft grunt in the back of her throat paired with the way she melted against me, parting her lips and plunging her tongue into my mouth.

Something inside me roared in a victorious growl like I was conquering her. My hands slid into her hair, still as thick and soft as it ever was, and she whimpered, winding her arms around my neck.

I didn't know what to touch first. It was like a starving man in front of a feast, my head spinning at all the abundance in front of me. Her ass was just as firm and ripe as I remembered. I sunk my fingers into her flesh while she moaned into my mouth, going with it when I lifted her onto the counter. She parted her legs for me, and fuck, was there anything more gratifying than that? Then she silently welcomed me in, drawing me closer, locking her legs around me so I could grind against her pussy.

"Evan..." she whispered when I touched my lips to her throat, lapping at her silky skin.

How was it so soft? Every swipe of my tongue left her gasping, clinging to me, hands pulling my shirt free from my waistband. With a grunt, I helped her, almost tearing the damn thing off. I was that hungry for her touch. I needed to feel her hands on me, *all over* me.

I needed to be surrounded by her. My skin sizzled, and my dick strained against the zipper as I slid my hands under her sweatshirt, lifting it over her head. This was fucking crazy, but I couldn't stop. For years, I'd held myself back, wanting her. I didn't realize how much until now, until everything I had missed for so long was here in my arms, grinding against me, urging me on with every soft moan and helpless whimper.

Lowering my head, I lifted one of her full tits to my mouth so I could worship it the way she deserved. "Oh, just like that," she begged while her fingers clawed through my hair. A string of guttural moans filled the air and made my ears ring.

It was the same but different. We had both grown up, and in her case, that meant demanding what she wanted. "Suck harder," she whispered, breathlessly. "It's not...fuck, make it hurt. Make me feel something..." Her words transformed into a moan when I caught her taut nipple between my teeth and flicked the tip with my tongue. Her legs tightened around my hips, her hips jerking until the friction was enough to make me press against her harder, demanding.

"What do you need from me?" I whispered, teasing her nipples with my thumbs until she whined in frustration. It was beyond gratifying, like some erotic fantasy come to life, having this gorgeous, sensual creature under my control.

The wild, sexy teenager had turned into a sensual woman I couldn't wait to claim. "Do you want my cock? Do you want me inside you?"

"Oh, God..." her head rolled from one side to the other, eyes closed, "... you're killing me. I want..."

"Tell me." I drove myself against her again, torturing both of us with the friction. "I can't give you what you want unless you tell me what it is, Valentina."

"Fuck me!" She whined, making me chuckle. I had her where I wanted her, on the edge of her control, unwilling to give in to me but without a choice.

"Good girl," I praised, lifting her off the counter with her body still wrapped around mine.

Neither of us said a word while I carried her up the stairs, her face buried in my neck, her tongue tracing my earlobe and jaw. I could barely think or hardly breathe. I only knew what I needed, and that was the complete obliteration only she could grant. Only she ever had.

I wasn't graceful, falling onto the bed with her once I reached it. "Take what you want," I invited, groaning when her writhing body rubbed against my aching bulge. "Let me watch you put on a show for me."

She straddled me, her pussy grinding against my covered cock. Her thighs were so silky, inviting my hands to move higher until they were inside her shorts and caressing her ass. She sucked in a gasp, lifting momentarily, so I could drag them down along with her panties as I discarded them both to the floor. She rolled back over my bulging cock, and I ran my fingers up her thigh to her core.

God, she was soaked, and the finger I dragged through her slit left us both groaning helplessly. "Oh, God..." she moaned out, throwing her head back as I played with her hot, slick pussy. I could've watched her all night, moving on top of me as I worked her into a frenzy while my dick dripped in anticipation.

She sat up all at once, lifting herself away from my throbbing length before finding my belt and unzipping my fly. I could only lie back and watch her, half in shadow, since only the downstairs lights were on. Somehow, that added to the thrill.

My hand shook with urgency as I pulled my wallet from my back pocket to take out a foil-wrapped condom.

The touch of her slim fingers around my throbbing shaft damn near wiped every conscious thought out of my mind. How could I think with pure sensation invading every aspect of my being? I could hardly breathe, and I sure as hell couldn't think about anything but the pleasure threatening to tear my mind apart as Valentina unrolled the latex down my length.

How was it this good? How had it not been this good in years?

I took myself in one hand and dragged my head through her hot slit. She arched, going stiff, sucking in a sharp breath at the contact against her sensitive flesh. "Ready for this?" I whispered. "Are you ready for my cock inside you?"

"Y-yes!" she stuttered as I found her entrance and pulled her down until she enveloped me. Oh, fuck, she was still perfect. Tight, hot, made for me. She cried out, arching her back and pulling the clip from her hair, letting it hang free while she slid down my shaft.

I couldn't wait for her to adjust as I let out a guttural groan. I had waited ten fucking years, and now, with her hips in my hands, I thrust upward. It was magic, it was primal, it was something I didn't know how I lived without.

It took no time for her to set her pace, her hair brushing my chest when she leaned down to kiss me, riding me. "Fuck, yes," she whimpered out, grinding against my base while her head swung back and forth in abandon.

I was on fire. Her touch, those hands all over my skin, nails scraping my shoulders and chest. Her cunt tightened, greedy for my cock, threatening to milk me dry.

More than anything, it was her. Valentina. Wild, untethered, leaning down so she could whisper in my ear. "You feel so good. So good..." I thrust upward to meet her strokes, and she shivered, her moans turning to high-pitched whines. She was close, clenching around me, threatening to make me explode.

"Come for me," I growled into her ear. "Cream on my cock."

All at once, the tension broke, her ecstatic cries filling my ears. That was my sign to let go. When I did, it was with a roar so intense it left my head spinning. *Holy fuck.* She was still spasming around me by the time she lifted her hips to let me slip from her, soft sighs coming with every heaving breath she took.

After disposing of the condom in a wastebasket next to the bed, I flopped onto my back. I was wiped out but euphoric after coming harder than I had in ages. What made it better was the way she sighed beside me before curling up with her head on my shoulder. "That wasn't bad for round one," she murmured, and I'd be damned if my dick didn't twitch in response.

~

THE COLD LIGHT of morning had a way of changing things.

She was fast asleep, snoring softly when I sat up, surrounded by pillows and twisted sheets we'd left behind before passing out.

What were we supposed to do now? What was I supposed to do? I was never any good at words, and she deserved something, anything. What would I say?

She slept peacefully, her bare skin glowing like a pearl in the light filtering through the curtains, her hair a chocolate brown fan across the white pillowcase. After three rounds last night, it was no wonder she was out cold. When she woke, there'd be the awkward small talk, possibly resentment.

Worse yet... regret.

But I couldn't leave without watching her one last time, gently running the back of my hand across her warm, rosy cheek and memorizing her timeless beauty from up close.

Déjà vu is a motherfucker. *Suddenly, we were eighteen again, and she had fallen asleep in my room, exhausted from too many orgasms. I found myself admiring her swollen lips and dark lashes atop the apples of her cheeks before gently wrapping a sheet around her to keep her warm.*

Just as quickly, I pushed away the memories as they came flooding in and removed my hand.

She would call me a coward, and maybe I was tiptoeing downstairs to grab the rest of my clothes and clean up the cold food I'd left on the counter. The thought of leaving her a note crossed my mind, but I pushed it down. It wasn't like we'd never see each other again.

She'd thank me for this. Making a clean break.

At least, that's what I told myself. I needed to believe it by the time I crept out of the silent apartment, hoping she'd understand.

3

VALENTINA

"We'll set some dates at this meeting, and I'll forward you the info as soon as I have it." Traffic on 495 was light, meaning I could make good time on my way out to East Hampton the Monday after Rose's engagement party.

We needed to hit the ground running on this, so I had my assistant already compiling potential vendor information and combing through lists of vendors we had partnered with in the past in hopes they'd be willing to do us a favor and rush a project. With all the events I'd planned and publicized, it meant having a deep well to draw from.

Bianca's soft sigh didn't give me much confidence. "It's the second week in April already," she reminded me.

"No kidding. That's why the temperatures have been warming up."

"I'm just saying. It would be one thing if a short timeline meant, like, September. We could handle that. But we're heading into wedding season as it is."

"You're not telling me anything I don't already know," I assured her. She was an amazing assistant, but she had a habit of stating the obvious when I was already three steps ahead of her. Then again, I'd had nothing but time yesterday to stew over after waking up alone in my messy bed.

It's for the best. I had spoken those words to myself so many times over the course of a rainy Sunday that they popped into my head before I could help it. It *was* for the best that he left. I wouldn't have known what to say. *Sorry, I needed something to take the pain away, and alcohol didn't work.* Yeah, no, even if it was the sad truth.

Things would be awkward enough the next time we saw each other, whenever that happened to be. No doubt it would be something wedding-related. My stomach felt a little queasy when I considered that. There would be plenty of things to do in the weeks leading up to the wedding, and of course, Colton would want Evan to be part of it.

Would anybody mind if I took a break from group functions for the rest of the summer?

"Did you hear me? Am I breaking up?" Bianca asked, raising her voice until it filled the inside of my Mercedes.

"You did cut out a little," I lied, too busy thinking about the mistake I made two nights ago. "Run that by me again?"

"I said, my biggest concern is finding a venue. I mean, anybody with availability at this point is probably available because nobody wants them."

"One thing at a time," I urged. My head was starting to hurt. "Let me make this meeting, and I'll fill you in as soon as I leave. Until then, take a breath and maybe a Valium."

Ending the call, I took a breath of my own, then another, fighting to calm my nerves. It wasn't the wedding on my mind. That I could plan and execute a showstopper on short notice in my sleep.

How could he have left without saying a word? No note, no

text, nothing. All he'd done was clean up after we left the food lying out.

Was I surprised? I knew better than to expect anything from him. He had already disappointed me once. Maybe the worst a person could be. More than that, he never apologized. Why apologize now for punking out on me like he had? Time hadn't granted him the balls to own up to the things he did.

It shouldn't have come as a surprise, yet I couldn't keep the memories and the subsequent letdown from playing on a never-ending loop.

There was a hell of a lot more going on in my life than screwing up and fucking Evan. My stupid body insisted on reminding me how good it was—maybe the best ever, and that wasn't an exaggeration. I didn't want it to be true. I wanted the sex to be forgettable, for it to fade into the background of my memory the way other partners had. But no, the idiot had to go and make me come three times, and hard enough that I basically passed out in the end.

Was it wrong that I wanted it again?

Of course, it was. Terribly so, not to mention incredibly stupid. Sure, why not walk headfirst into a mistake? And that's what it would have been. Because I knew him, and I knew what was waiting for me if I let myself get involved. It was one thing for a naïve, eighteen-year-old kid to fall for a boy who broke her heart. I was twenty-eight now, and my eyes were wide-fucking-open.

I was grateful when my exit came up. It meant I could busy my mind with something productive instead of the downward spiral I was heading.

Arriving at the store was a breath of fresh air. Rose and Colton had worked so hard to turn an old bank into a showplace featuring Farrah Goldsmith couture. Stepping inside, I found a handful of women my mother's age talking with one of the stylists while preparing for some big event.

I headed straight back to Rose's office, tapping on the closed door and waiting for her to call out. "Yes?"

"Just me." I stepped into the cozy space and closed the door, cutting off the overlapping voices outside. "No offense, but you don't look so great."

"I feel even worse than I look." She pushed her chair back from the desk and reached between her calves, holding up a wastebasket for me to see. "Just in case I have to hurl."

"Oh, I'm sorry. Poor thing." Funny, but I could handle talking about the baby now. It was just the shock on Saturday night that had me reeling and making incredibly unwise decisions. That was all. "Do you want me to go out and, I don't know, get you ginger ale or something? Saltines?"

"I already have a sleeve of crackers, and this is ginger ale in my cup." She held up a pink tumbler, sipping from the straw. "I can't let it paralyze me, and they say it only lasts a little while. Not the whole nine months."

I dropped into a chair on the other side of her desk and set my bag on the floor at my feet. "That's good. So hopefully, by the time the wedding comes, this part will have passed."

"Fingers crossed. So, since we're on the subject..."

"Yes. The wedding you got me to agree to plan without telling me you were pregnant."

She winced, briefly closing her eyes. "I know, I know. I should have mentioned it. But we wanted to wait until it seemed like everything was okay. You know?"

I knew very well, and the knowledge was a fist clenching my heart until it ached. "So what are we thinking?" I asked, pulling out my tablet and stylus to take notes. "Have you thought about dates?"

"I've thought about not wanting to look like a whale in my wedding gown," she explained with a grimace. "Which means it needs to be, like, soon. *Very soon.*"

"How soon are we talking?" I asked while my heart threatened to crawl up into my throat.

"I'm around twelve weeks now. I haven't popped or anything, and I read it can take longer to show with the first baby. So maybe another... two months? At the most?" Her shoulders hunched up around her ears, cringing like she was waiting for me to hit her.

Two months. While it wasn't really a surprise, I was hoping for a little more time. Would it have been so much to ask? "Okay," I murmured, pulling up a calendar to look for dates.

"It's impossible, isn't it?" she fretted. "I knew it would be."

One thing I knew about pregnant women was that it was a good idea to keep them calm whenever possible. "Hey. I've got this. Or have you completely lost faith in me?" I questioned.

Only a touch of the strain on her face melted away. "I know how incredible you are, but I know there's no such thing as actual miracles."

"You might be surprised." Did I mean a word of what I said? No way. Inside, I was shaking, even panicking a little. Two months tops when June was the busiest month for weddings as it was. Two months to pull off something great, something worthy of the names Black and Goldsmith.

Money wouldn't be an issue. That much I knew for sure. Ari Goldsmith would spare no expense to make sure his daughter had the wedding of her dreams. And anything he couldn't or wouldn't provide, Barrett Black definitely would. I didn't think that would be an issue, though. Not when it came to the apple of Ari's eye. But money could only get me so far, even with the inevitable rush fees I would pay.

What I couldn't do was free up a ballroom already taken by another party. In the end, that would be my biggest concern. Where to have the damn thing. "Are you set on Manhattan?" I asked. It wasn't easy to sound casual, even as I crossed my fingers and hoped for the answer I needed.

"Oh, no. If anything, I would like to have it somewhere outside of town. Maybe out here, Martha's Vineyard, Cape Cod. That sort of thing. I'm open to all sorts of ideas." Tapping her chin, she added, "It sucks they're doing work up at the estate until July, or I would say we could hold it there. That's where my parents had their wedding."

"Right. Something about replacing the old windows?" I asked, vaguely recalling overhearing Mom chatting it over with Olivia.

"And the roof needs fixing on the east side," she confirmed with a sigh. "That storm we had a couple of weeks ago did damage to some of the shingles. It's an old place."

What exquisite timing. Even Mother Nature wanted to throw me a curveball. I smiled through my growing panic. "That's because there's another even more perfect place out there. And I'll find it. I'll have Bianca start making calls right now." I pulled out my phone to send her a text, which would only make her blood pressure shoot through the roof. At least she could freak out while I was two hours away and might have the worst of it out of her system by the time I returned.

"Hey, I heard there's a wedding planning meeting going on." Colton's deep voice rang through the room before he entered, carrying a small bag with a pharmacy logo stamped on the front. "Your nausea pills," he announced, holding up the bag like a trophy.

"The doctor prescribed them..." Rose explained. "But I didn't really need them filled until now. It seems like it's getting worse." They shared a kiss before Colton popped the bottle open and tipped a pill into her open palm. It was little gestures like that that warmed my heart.

They also left me feeling a little bit jealous, and that wasn't like me.

Damn Evan.

Damn past.

Damn inability to move on the way I thought I had after a handful of relationships and many more casual flings that went nowhere.

"How's it going?" Colton asked me. "What do you think? Can we pull it off?"

"I think it's cute that you use the word *we*," I retorted, sticking out my tongue. "But yeah. It'll be totally fine. I know what I'm doing. Don't you worry."

Rose couldn't let it go because that wasn't how she did things. "I'm just worried there won't be any place available. Tell me the truth. Are we going to end up having this at a Taco Bell or something?"

"I was thinking McDonald's," I countered. "They still have those Playland things for kids, right? With the slides and whatnot. So, we have entertainment for the young ones."

"That's what you're worried about?" Colton perched on the corner of the desk, shrugging. "Why don't we ask Evan? He is running, what, three of the family's country clubs now? Four? I lost count."

Funny how Evan never offered that the other night when I

mentioned how stressed I was about a venue. It confirmed what I already knew. He would always make himself the priority.

Rose's eyes lit up while my stomach dropped. If things got much worse, it would be me sitting with a wastebasket between my legs. "Sure. I could call him," I offered, since what else was I supposed to do? Rose was pleading with me, hanging on my every word like they were her lifeline.

"I know he could make it work. He's got what? There's one on the Vineyard. There's the one in Greenwich..." He held up two fingers. "Or are there two on the Vineyard? Fuck, I've lost track."

"I'll call him," I repeated. Did I sound a little sharp? Maybe. Maybe the idea of having to talk to Evan after he snuck off on me made me feel a little sharp.

Then again, what the hell was I thinking? This was good. I doubted he would have any availability, but I would try anyway because I'd be damned if he would get away with sneaking out with no explanation.

I didn't exactly want one. I only wanted him to squirm a little. That was the least he owed me.

"I'll step out right now and give him a call," I offered, already halfway out of my chair. "Be right back."

My legs trembled as I left the office, exiting through the back door that opened onto a small parking lot. I wasn't sure what I wanted the answer to be as I pulled up Evan's contact in my phone. Yes, it would make life a hell of a lot easier if he had an available date that fell within Rose's timeframe. Did I want a reason to have to spend time with him, though? Things hadn't exactly gone spectacularly on Saturday, orgasms aside.

Part of me didn't expect him to answer, the coward. But he did, and only after one ring. "Hey. I'm glad you called," he said before I had the chance to speak. "I was hoping you would."

Why did his voice have to sound so warm, rich, and friendly? *Intimate.* And why didn't it make me feel uncomfortable? No, the opposite was true. My chest warmed, and a smile tipped the corners of my mouth.

Until I remembered what a cowardly little prick he was for running out. "Well, I'd like to say I wanted to make sure you were still alive... like you weren't captured or something. Sucked up into the sky."

"No, I'm still here on solid ground. Listen—"

"There's no time for that. There's no time for much of anything," I said, interrupting and closing my eyes, crossing my fingers. "We're in a jam here. I've got eight weeks to make this wedding happen, tops. I have no clue how I'm supposed to make it all work, but I'll figure it out. The only thing I'm concerned with is the venue. Colton suggested I call you to see if you have any availability at one of your country clubs."

"Eight weeks." He blew out a soft whistle that had a strange effect on me.

I didn't love the idea of making a hundred phone calls, begging for a favor, basically crawling on my belly and promising the world to whoever would let us hold the wedding under their roof. But considering the effect Evan's voice had on me when he first answered my call, begging for favors and crawling on my belly sounded like it might be the safer bet.

"Give me a second." I heard him typing in the background.

Please, please. Only, what was I silently praying for? The best for Rose and Colton. That was what mattered. Not my heart, not my past, certainly not my body. Or his. Or what they did when they got together.

"Dammit," he growled out. "I forgot they're upgrading the booking system, so I can't access the full calendar of events at all locations right now."

"My luck continues to improve," I groaned out.

"Why don't you come out to the Greenwich office tomorrow?" he suggested. "The system will be up and running. I'm sure we can make something work."

A face-to-face meeting tomorrow. I started the call, determined to make him squirm, yet I was the one who suddenly felt all hot and itchy at the idea of being in the same room with him.

Somebody up there was having the laugh of the century at my expense.

"Sounds good, if you can swing it," I offered. "It's short notice and all."

"I'll make time for you," he promised. How could such a simple statement make my insides go warm and liquid while freezing my heart solid?

He hadn't made time for me when I'd needed him the most.

4

EVAN

"Next weekend, we have the McConnell and Latimer weddings on Saturday and Sunday, respectively." My events coordinator released a soft sigh as she scrolled through the calendar on her phone. "Friday night is the engagement party for the Jacobson wedding we have booked in October. That's here in Greenwich."

I was only half listening to Serena as she went over our upcoming schedule for the next couple of weeks. Valentina was due to arrive any minute, and I had hoped to have this meeting finished by the time she showed up. There had to be time to clear my head a little since something about being around her fucked me up inside. Left me making idiotic choices.

"Let's finish this up later." I stood and buttoned my slate gray jacket, then straightened my dark blue tie. Blue like the color of Valentina's eyes. Right, because that was a thought I needed to have now or ever. "I have that meeting I scheduled yesterday. A last-minute thing."

"Right. The Goldsmith-Black wedding." When I arched

an eyebrow, Serena shrugged. "What? You put it on your calendar. Those are your friends, right?"

It was the perfect segue. "Yes, and that's why I'm going to handle all the details myself. I don't want you touching this one." Her lashes flitted, and I knew it came out wrong. "Not that I don't have faith in you," I added to placate her.

It seemed like I was always saying the wrong thing, especially here of late. My mouth moved before my brain could catch up.

"No, I get it." She made a note for herself. "It's a personal event. Hey, I'm not going to complain about one less thing to worry about. I already have more than enough."

"Not exactly a bad thing," I reminded her, turning away from my desk to look out the window. The grounds of our adjoining golf course were a lush green, like an emerald carpet spreading out in front of me.

And it was mine.

I had taken this single country club that was given to me to run once I graduated with my business degree, and I purchased the golf course a year later. Two years after that, I purchased another three country clubs and poured money into renovating another two the family already owned that had been allowed to coast by on reputation for far too long. It wasn't long before I was given ownership of those locations as well.

Not yet thirty years old, I owned six extremely profitable country clubs, overseeing their management, the events held there, and the grounds. But it wasn't enough. I wanted more. I hadn't told anybody of my goal to have ten locations under my belt by the time my thirtieth birthday came along. Why ten? It was a nice, round number. Nothing more than that.

Expanding our private events' capabilities went a long

way toward our exploding profits. And a high-profile wedding like the one Ari was willing to pay for would draw hundreds and even thousands of interested eyes once photos spread online. Brides up and down the New England coast would claw each other to pieces if it meant holding their reception here.

Beyond that was the very real privilege of helping Colton. It wasn't like we sat around and talked about our feelings and shit like that, but I saw the effect Rose had on him. How much he wanted to make her happy. How happy she made him. They were proof it was possible to find something real.

If I could play a little part in that, I'd be glad to. I'd never say it out loud, but I would enjoy it.

Especially if it meant an excuse to be with Valentina.

My dick twitched at the thought of her. There I was thinking I had her out of my system years ago. All it took was one night to unravel all of that. We weren't exactly kids again—we never would be—but it didn't matter. Everything was still there.

The chemistry.

The connection.

And there was something that couldn't have existed back then when we were so young and only thought we knew anything about life. There was a difference between the sort of hot, animal fucking a pair of eighteen-year-olds could get down to and what adults could do after years of experience.

I was still lost in my thoughts when a knock at the door behind me pulled my head back to the present. Serena got up and answered, introducing herself before leading Valentina into the office.

· · ·

MY UNCLE OWNED a horse farm back when I was a kid, and I once spent a summer working for him. One hot day, the meanest, most ornery colt threw me from its back, and I hit the ground hard enough to knock the air from my lungs. It wasn't the way I always imagined it would feel, getting the wind knocked out of me. There was a helplessness to it, and it was fucking terrifying. A momentary flash of panicked certainty that I would never breathe again.

It wasn't a horse that threw me this time.

It was the tall, gorgeous brunette who entered my office like she belonged there. She scanned the room without reacting, flashing a brief, professional smile my way. "Good morning," she purred, or was that only in my head?

Everything she did was so fucking hot. I had trained myself out of looking at her like that from all the way back when I had a permanent hard-on for the sight of her ass. Obviously, there was no way we could coexist if I was drooling over her all the time.

I had to swallow the saliva that flooded my mouth as I took her in while she crossed the room. I hadn't expected the tailored suit she wore—a pale yellow that brought sunshine to mind and made her eyes look bluer in contrast. My hands clenched reflectively when I imagined unbuttoning her jacket, tearing off her white blouse, and opening the clip at the nape of her neck so her long, thick hair would tumble free.

The sight of my event coordinator's curious gaze brought me back to reality in a hurry. "Thanks, Serena," I murmured with a firm nod. "I'll catch you later, and we'll finish going over the calendar."

Valentina turned in a slow circle, surveying the room I'd carefully put together—modern, sleek, yet classic. Trends were a waste of money. "Can I get you something to drink?" I offered. "Coffee, maybe? We have a coffee bar on the premises, and they can whip up anything you like."

"I already caffeinated on the way here, but thanks," she demurred. We were alone now, but she maintained that standoffish approach, standing like a soldier ready for inspection.

"Are you hungry?" I asked. Why I was so damn determined to placate her, I had no idea.

"Trying to feed me again?" Her glossy lips tugged upward at the corners. At least she wasn't trying to pretend nothing happened or, worse, letting it get in the way of what we had to do. I should have known better than to think she would. She was a levelheaded, intelligent person, somebody who lived in the real world and understood how it worked.

I thought I was, too, though. The fact I couldn't keep my eyes off her legs as she took a seat across from my swivel chair left me questioning myself. Somehow, I managed to get together and offered, "Thank you for coming on such short notice."

"Thank you for meeting with me." She crossed her legs and balanced her tablet on her thigh, holding a stylus between her slim fingers. "So, did you have a chance to look at your calendars? See if you have anything available?"

Straight to business. Well, every day counted. It was probably a good thing she was focused. We could avoid the awkward chitchat.

I turned to my MacBook, plugging in dates and selecting all of our properties to cast a wide net. "Let me see. I have a Friday evening three weeks from now on the Vineyard."

"No way," she said with a laugh.

"Then there is a Sunday afternoon in Cape Cod on the following weekend, but I'm guessing an extra week still isn't enough time." A glance her way showed her shaking her head. "Otherwise, I have a Sunday, the first weekend in June. Here in Greenwich," I concluded. "What do you think? You're here, you've seen the place. I can take you on a tour if you want... show you the facilities. We could do a bachelor golf outing on Saturday... it looks like that afternoon is free."

"Slow down, slow down," she urged, taking notes. "Golf outing. I like it. What about locations in the area for lodging?"

"We've partnered with The Delamar and have connections to other hotels in the area," I told her. "I could reserve a block of rooms for the entire week if that's what we want. I'd have to make the calls soon, though."

"You've got all kinds of connections, haven't you?" There was admiration in her voice, even if it sounded a little bit patronizing.

"What? You think I sit around and do nothing but drink and order employees around all day? Of all people, you understand being able to pick up a phone and call in a favor when necessary. This will be a big one," I admitted. "With it only being around seven weeks out. But I think it's doable. If this was August and the leaf peepers were about to descend on us in weeks, it would be a different story."

Her face maintained its flat, professional expression. "Sounds good. What's the name of the managers there? Just so I know when I have to reach out to them."

She was determined to make this impersonal. That was fine with me. I only wished I could keep myself from lapsing into personal talk with her. Trying to make jokes, trying to make her smile. That was my role in our group, one I fell into easily.

Only she knew about the anxiety it stemmed from. It hadn't been easy trying to fit in with a bunch of trust fund babies back when I first started high school on an academic scholarship. I wore the uniform and attended classes, but I wasn't like them. My family was well-off, but we were nowhere near the kind of wealth families like the Diamonds and the Blacks took for granted. If I could make people laugh, I had a place. I felt like I belonged. In the early days, weeks, months, that was what I'd needed most. Over time, it became a habit.

After giving her the details of my contacts, I stood. "Let me show you around. Our ballroom can fit five hundred, though we could hold the ceremony and reception on the back lawn overlooking the golf course and lake. Do we have an idea of a guest list? Approximate number, at least?"

She followed me from my office and down the hall leading to a wide, sweeping staircase that led down to our elegant lobby. "I asked, and Rose said at least three hundred. Which probably means closer to four," she added with a wry grin. "There's nothing like planning a wedding to make a person remember a bunch of people they haven't spoken to in five years."

"Knowing Lourde and Olivia, I'm sure they'll come up with half of Manhattan and a third of East Hampton," I predicted.

We crossed the lobby and then passed a wall of windows overlooking the man-made lake that sat between the country club and golf course. It was large enough for small boats to sail, and a pair of sailboats bobbed on the sparkling surface. "It's gorgeous," she murmured, staring out, taking it all in. "I can see something really beautiful happening here."

I saw something beautiful in front of me, and I wasn't looking out the window. It was all wrong. I should have left her Saturday night. If I had tucked her into bed and shown myself out, I wouldn't now have to wrestle with the memory of her throaty moans. She was wild, uninhibited. I had already developed a taste for it. More like a craving if I were honest—a fast-growing need.

She noticed me ogling her and arched an eyebrow. If there was one thing she couldn't be bothered to do, it was pretending for the sake of politeness. "Is there a reason you keep staring at me like a deranged creeper on the subway? I'm waiting for you to flash me or something."

There was no way to answer that question without coming off like an idiot, so I chose to scoff. Turning away, I led her down the wide hall and into the ballroom. Crystal chandeliers hung overhead, lighting the room once I flipped the switches before crossing the polished parquet floor to open the drapes covering the French doors that overlooked the formal gardens, which would be in bloom by early June.

She whistled softly, admiring the room, tipping her head back to check out the high ceiling. "This is stunning. I mean it. I'm impressed."

"Thank you. I'm pretty proud of it," I admitted. "What do you think? Will this be enough for the wedding of the year?"

"You know it will," she quipped, rolling her eyes at me from across the room. "I'm not trying to stroke your ego when you know damn well this would make the site of a gorgeous wedding. Do you think we could leave the doors open so guests could go in and out during the reception?" she asked, approaching me and bringing the scent of lilacs with her. Was it her hair or perfume? Regardless, it was intoxicating.

"I don't see why not. We could have the grounds decorated. We could even have a second band outside, under a marquee. Lay down a dance floor, providing an alternative to whatever is being played inside."

For the first time since she showed up, she wore a

genuine smile. Her shoulders sank in time with a deep sigh. "This is going to be special," she murmured, and I believed her. Not because Ari could afford it or because I could help provide it. I believed it because she did.

"I trust your judgment," I told her, staring at the flutter on the side of her throat where her pulse throbbed. I had licked that patch of skin and remembered the taste clearly enough that a wave of hunger threatened to knock me on my ass or force me to reach for her, which I knew instinctively she would punish me for. This wasn't the time to fuck around or lose sight of what we were here to do. It was too damn complicated. The past was bad enough without dredging it up all because she made my dick hard.

"You trust my judgment, but you couldn't trust me enough to stick around on Sunday morning?" She leveled me with a hard, unblinking stare.

I should've fucking known she'd bring it up. It had all been too easy. "Why do I feel like this is a trap?" I asked. Any softness or warmth was history, and maybe that was a good thing. I needed to be reminded it was a mistake to sleep with her again. "I thought we were here to talk about business."

"How convenient for you." She sighed.

"You want to talk about it? Fine. Maybe I knew you would regret what happened as soon as you opened your eyes, and I didn't want to be around when it happened. I didn't want to make you feel awkward, and I sure as hell didn't want you to feel like you had to apologize for making a move. I was trying to be decent."

"Yeah, well, you missed the mark just a little." Valentina held her thumb and forefinger roughly an inch apart, scowling. "It was kind of shitty. I'm not some skank you sneak away from the morning after."

"I know you aren't. That's not how I see you."

"The fact is, I needed a friend that night, and you were there, and I appreciate it." Had she rehearsed this? It sure as hell poured out of her mouth like she had. "But I think it would be best if we go back to the way things were before."

"Of course." All that was left to do was hide a flash of bitter disappointment. It was ridiculous to feel that way. Treating Saturday like a one-off and moving on with our lives was the way to go. For one, there wouldn't be this awkwardness where she couldn't look me in the eye for long before needing to look away. It was better to move on.

I cleared my throat, nodding toward the lake. "We could set up sailing for the ladies the day before the wedding," I suggested. "I don't know if you've ever been to the spa at the Delamar, but it's huge. The girls could have a spa day there. I'm spitballing," I concluded with a shrug.

"I like the way your brain works." She liked the way my dick worked too. Fuck, how was I supposed to think about headcounts and all that shit when I couldn't look at her without remembering the way she tipped her head back in abandon when I thrust deep inside her?

"I can set up consultations with our food services manager and our pastry chef," I suggested, pulling out my phone to check my calendar and rid myself of images of her. "I can juggle a few things in my schedule to make room since this is all rushed."

"You?" Her forehead wrinkled when she frowned. "What about the girl upstairs? Serena? She said she was your event coordinator."

"I've already told Serena I'm handling this one myself."

A shadow passed over her face but vanished quickly. "Okay," she said with a shrug. "Whatever you think is best.

I'm too grateful to question anything you have to say right now."

"Careful," I warned. "Say that kind of thing to the wrong guy, and you might regret it."

One eyebrow slowly arched, her pouty lips pursing. "And what makes you the right guy?" she countered.

God, those lips. That delicious mouth. "I never said I was," I whispered, staring while the devil on my shoulder pointed out how easy it would be to lean down and taste her again.

She stiffened, then backed away. "I've seen all I need to. I'm going to get on Rose and Colton to firm up their guest list by the end of the week and rush print on invites."

The moment was over. In the end, it was not a bad thing, though I fought a deflated feeling as I closed the drapes. "I'll reach out with menu info," I offered. "We'll have to keep in close touch."

She snickered, turning on her heel and striding across the empty floor. Damn, her ass was a work of art I couldn't help staring at. "This isn't my first rodeo, cowboy."

5

VALENTINA

"Who's ready for another mimosa?" Olivia Goldsmith held up a pitcher of orange juice, which was sitting on ice, along with a pair of champagne bottles and, beside it, an assortment of treats, savory and sweet. The sight of the sumptuous spread laid out on the table at the Goldsmith flagship store made my mouth water. Ari had given us free rein to go through their bridal collection and pull any pieces we liked.

"Rose, honey? Do you need more ginger ale?" Rose shook her head while a pair of stylists attached clips to the back of a stunning but simple ivory gown. The gown's empire waist and full skirt flattered her slightly fuller figure. Her preference had been a form-fitting mermaid silhouette, but she didn't want even the slightest baby bump to appear larger in a tight dress.

ARIA OPENED the dressing room curtain and stepped out, wearing a peach chiffon dress with the hem skimming the floor. "I like the little capelet," she announced, playing with the transparent layer of chiffon skimming her shoulders and chest. "It'll help me cover these flabby arms."

"Shut up." Sienna laughed. "There's not an ounce of flab on you, girl." She twirled in front of a mirror, wearing a silk, navy strapless tea-length whose hem fell below her knee.

"I like them both so much." Rose sighed, looking from Sienna to Aria in the mirror while Olivia and Lourde fussed like the mothers they were, tearing up almost as much as the hormonal bride-to-be. "How am I supposed to choose? And when are you going to try something on?" she demanded, finding me in the mirror.

"Hello? My twin is right here. And we are the same size. Whatever looks good on her will look good on me." A bridesmaid's dress was the least of my worries.

"It is so refreshing to see a bride worried about how her bridesmaids feel in their dresses," Sienna pointed out as she poured herself another mimosa.

"Right?" Aria giggled on her way back to her dressing room, where another pair of dresses waited to be tried on. "Remember Penelope Schwartz's wedding? Those poor girls looked like they were on their way to a costume party where the theme was *tacky*."

"I'm pretty sure she's been the worst since the day she was born," I agreed, only half listening while typing an email to a florist I was determined to work with on this. There would be more than one as I had a big vision in mind, and there would be no way to pull it off in such a short amount of time without extra hands and resources.

"The marriage only lasted, what? A year?" Rose sounded sincerely sad, even a little emotional. "Nobody imagines their marriage will only last a year when they're trying on their dresses, you know?"

Sienna had gotten her cue, appearing at Rose's side,

holding out a pack of tissues. "Those damn hormones," she murmured as Rose pulled a tissue from the pack and dabbed at her eyes.

"I'm sorry," she mumbled before laughing shakily. "I can't get a hold of myself."

"It must be pretty bad if you're tearing up over Penelope, of all people." I stood beside her once the stylists stepped back and smiled at her reflection. "What do you think? How do you feel in this?"

"I feel like a bride," she whispered, smiling through the tears that still sparkled in her eyes. "I can't shake the feeling I should pinch myself."

"Look out, everybody." Aria flung the curtain open again, this time wearing a tight-fitting pink dress that barely reached her knees and fit her like a glove.

Rose whistled in appreciation. "You look hot, but you're not allowed to look better than the bride."

"Honey, nobody will be able to take their eyes off you," Aria promised, tugging the hemline self-consciously before yanking the bodice up to cover more of her boobs. "I couldn't wear this. I'd be fidgeting the whole day."

"Miles would like it," I teased. It was fun to watch her blush, and it only deepened when she glanced toward the older women hovering nearby. Their relationship was still new enough, and the memory of her hating him was still fresh enough that I could enjoy giving her shit over falling for somebody she was determined to hate when they first met. Considering they were now on the verge of moving into his new penthouse together, that attitude hadn't lasted very long.

It occurred to me as the moms gathered close and praised Rose that I was the only single girl left in the group. Not that I was in any hurry to settle down. It would take someone with a lot of patience to handle a girlfriend whose job meant she spent most of her time at clubs, bars, and parties she promoted. It meant constantly being surrounded by men, with most of them drunk or on their way there by the time we crossed paths. It was a recipe for tension, and who wanted to deal with that?

"I think this is the one." Rose stared back at her reflection and wore a shy little smile as she turned away from the mirror, arms spread. The sweetheart neckline and thin straps showed off her creamy decolletage and toned shoulders to perfection, and her peaches and cream complexion glowed against the ivory silk. But that probably had something to do with the pregnancy. She had that special glow going on no matter what she wore.

"You're radiant, darling," Olivia whispered, her throat clogged with emotion while Aunt Lourde hugged her, also crying.

It was a lot easier getting out of the gown than it was getting her into it. Pretty soon, she was sitting on a sofa, sipping flat ginger ale while we discussed our choice of bridesmaid dresses.

"You really should try the peach one on," Lourde urged, holding it out to me now that Aria had taken it off. "I want to see it on you." Rose nodded her agreement, and I didn't want to make the bride unhappy. I took the dress and ducked into one of the dressing rooms, closing the curtain before taking off my jacket and the sundress underneath it.

"You said something about a cake tasting next weekend," Aria said, and I assumed she was talking to Rose. "Are you going to have time for that? Do you need one of us to go in your place since you're so busy at the store?"

"Valentina is already on it," Rose announced. I couldn't see her, but I could hear the smile in her voice. "We owe

Evan so much for riding his team like he is, getting everything in place."

The sound of his name tightened my nipples. That was all it took, just hearing his name mentioned in a casual conversation. Goose bumps rose over my arms and shoulders, but that could easily have been the air conditioning vent over my head. *Sure. Air conditioning. A likely story.*

"Is he giving you shit?" Sienna called out to me.

No, he gave me his dick. I grinned. Right. That announcement would go well. "No," I replied as I stepped into a puddle of peach chiffon and slid it up over my body. "Honestly, he's been great. He doesn't keep me waiting for a response to questions, he's proactive in coming up with solutions to problems. He knows his stuff."

"Coming from you, that's a huge compliment," Rose declared. "I don't think I trust anybody's judgment the way I trust yours."

If she only knew how shitty my judgment had been lately. Still, it had been two weeks since I slept with Evan, and the world hadn't come tumbling down. He was behaving himself, keeping it professional in our emails and brief phone calls. I had the sense there was as much riding on this for him as there was for me. He wanted to do a good job for his best friend. I might still have wrestled with mixed feelings toward him, but I wouldn't let him cloud my opinion.

There was a chance we could move on from this with no repercussions or complications. I needed to believe that, or else I had opened myself up to a world of bullshit there was no time to deal with.

"You know," Aria said, her voice closer, as if she were standing just on the other side of the curtain. "If you need any help at all, I'm here. I don't think Mom would miss me at the foundation if I told her I was helping you with the wedding planning and stuff."

Something in her voice made me pause before pushing back the curtain. It was only a matter of time before she started worrying about me. I was amazed she had waited this long before saying anything. On the surface, her offer came across as one sister trying to help another, but I knew better.

I pulled back my shoulders and forced a smile. "I'll let you know if I need your help," I told her, brushing past her on my way to the three-way mirror. "I really, really do like this," I announced, checking myself out from all angles. "It's so pretty. Do you still want those flowered combs for our hair?" I asked Rose.

"Yes, for sure. I want everything to look romantic and soft and lush." Her voice had a dreamy sound to it, and I knew she would shit a brick when she saw what I had in mind for the ballroom. It was sort of a surprise, something I had seen done at an event in Virginia and wanted to recreate.

"Really," Rose continued as she stood, looking and sounding stronger than before. "We could try for the rest of our lives, and we would never be able to thank you and Evan enough for all the extra time you're putting into this. It means everything." She gave me a hug before I reached the dressing room to change into my clothes.

"No tears," I murmured, chuckling when she sniffled. "We got you. Everything is going to be incredible. All you have to do is look gorgeous, which you do every day anyway."

"Are you so nice to all of your clients?"

"Only the ones I love." I gave her a wink before disappearing behind the curtain and releasing a soft sigh.

It wasn't easy keeping up appearances. Not that the wedding was a problem. Aside from the planning being so damn hectic, it couldn't have gone better. I normally had to poke and prod vendors on a rush job like this, but Evan was on top of everything. I typically hated being cc'd on emails but actually enjoyed witnessing the way he interacted with members of his staff. He was firm but fair. He didn't threaten or force the way shitty leaders tended to do. I was seeing a new side of him, and it was... nice.

"I better run. As much as I want to hang out with you girls all day..." Sienna was gathering her things when I opened the curtain, the peach dress hanging over my arm. "I have a lunch meeting in twenty."

"Another client in trouble?" Aria guessed.

"I swear, I don't know whether to laugh or cry sometimes. No matter how I tell people to behave themselves, they do whatever the hell they want." Sienna shrugged, smirking before she went to her mom for a quick hug. "Then again, would I have a job otherwise? I guess I can't really complain."

We made plans for dress fittings in a couple of weeks before she scurried off, followed by Lourde and Olivia. "I'm going to head over to the apartment with Mom," Rose announced. "Dad will be happy to know we found dresses today. He's so stressed, you would think it was *his* wedding all over again."

"He wants everything to be perfect. Tell him it will," I reminded her before she left the dressing area.

That meant Aria and I were on our own. "Want to grab some lunch?" she asked, lingering in the doorway leading out to the showroom.

"I wish I could, but I have to check in at the office," I told her.

"On a Saturday?" She sighed.

"I've been too distracted by this project to pay attention to everything else we have going on, and Bianca's going to wring my neck if I don't answer some questions she has."

"A quick coffee?" she offered.

I narrowed my eyes at my sister, concerned. "Are you all right? Do you need to talk? I have all the time in the world if you do." Work could wait.

"Oh, no!" She shook her head hard, laughing softly. "No, everything's great. Like, really great. It's..." She trailed off, biting her lip. "It's you I want to talk about. I want to make sure *you're* okay."

I knew it was too good to be true—to have a day where everyone would focus anywhere but on me. "Why wouldn't I be?" I asked, scrolling through a couple of new emails that had come in while I was trying on my dress.

"Could you put the phone down for a second and actually look at me? I'm standing right here in front of you."

Lowering the phone, I sighed. "I'm just fine," I insisted, although it took considerable effort to keep from sounding as annoyed as I felt. "A little overwhelmed with all this work, but things are going better than I expected."

"That's not answering my question, and you know it. Did you forget who you're talking to?" she whispered when I rolled my eyes. "This is me. I want to know about you, *my sister*. Not the girl planning this wedding. Are you all right with all of this?"

I didn't have time to be coy, and my patience was alarmingly thin. Rather than pretend I didn't know what she meant, I shrugged. "I don't know what you want me to say."

"I want you to say you aren't as stricken and devastated as you looked at the engagement party. It's okay to hurt," she assured me, but I couldn't help but scoff and roll my eyes.

"But when you pretend you aren't hurting, that's when problems start."

"I know that!" I replied. It wasn't easy not to flip her off and storm out. "I honestly don't know why you're so worried. It came as a shock. It set me off after I'd already had a few drinks. It's over."

Her teeth sank into her lip. "You know why. I'm only concerned about you."

"And I appreciate that, but you don't need to be. I'm okay."

"So I was imagining things when you looked like you were going to burst into tears?"

"Can we not talk about that? That was two damn weeks ago," I hissed out. "And it's over now. Yeah, it sort of surprised me in a bad way, but I'm over it. Let me be over it." It wasn't until I said it out loud that I understood how much I needed to move on. To put it behind me *again*. I couldn't spend the rest of my life crying over something that happened so long ago. There was no way to change it, like there was no way to go back and slap the shit out of Evan for letting me down.

That still wasn't enough for her. She opened her mouth, but I held up a hand, scowling. "You promised me we would never talk about it. Remember? Not ever. It's over."

"You honestly believe that? We are not kids anymore," she reminded me. "That's the kind of thing a kid says and actually believes. This is real life. We can't run away from the things that hurt."

"Thank you very much for your advice." This was getting to be too much. I had to leave before I said something I couldn't take back. Not all of us were lucky enough to find the perfect person. "I really have to go, or else Bianca's head is going to explode, and I don't feel like having to clean that up." I gave her a quick kiss on the cheek, making my escape before she could try to stop me.

～

"We couldn't have done this without you." Hunt Kennedy, the owner of Club Urge, raised his glass to me, his leg brushing mine when he angled his body toward me on his barstool. The club was packed on a Saturday night, only a little more than a month after it opened. There had been a dozen obstacles in my way, including the complete irresponsibility of the man now toasting me, but I had made it work despite him.

From then on, I would not trust a client to get their permits arranged in time for opening. Lesson learned.

I laughed off the compliment, holding my glass high. "You must know what you're doing because you're packing them in." Somebody bumped me from behind and almost made me spill my martini, but I recovered quickly and laughed it off.

"You're pretty fucking cool," he announced, narrowing his steely eyes. He was hot in a dangerous, you-might-wake-up-to-find-your-wallet-missing sort of way. "Nothing throws you off, does it? You're, like, made of ice."

It was what I wanted people to believe. The truth was different, but people weren't interested in the truth. That had always been my experience anyway. The illusion was much more interesting. Safer too. "You have to be when you do this kind of work," I told him.

Lowering his brow, he growled out, "I bet I could get you to melt."

That was surprising. There had never been anything flirtatious between us, but then we had been working on promoting the club's opening. That was over now, and it seemed like he took it as a green light to try his luck. I could feel his lustful gaze crawling over me, and while I wasn't turned off, it didn't get me excited either. I may as well have been dead below the waist.

Get it together. He's hot. He's available. And he's eye fucking you at this very moment. Yes, and I could have used a good, hard fuck after two weeks of longing for what had exploded between Evan and me. Two frustrated weeks full of dirty dreams and an overworked vibrator. I was just as frustrated as ever. He could be a lot of fun, and he might have made it possible for me to put Evan behind me and move on.

No matter how hard I tried, I couldn't imagine it. Maybe I didn't want to. "You know," I said before downing the rest of my martini. "I wouldn't be any good tonight. It's been an extremely long week, and I'm exhausted. But thanks for the offer," I added when he scowled.

"Yeah, sure. Have fun tonight." Just like that, he was gone, probably in search of a willing pussy after being turned down.

I was in trouble. I had to get past this. Otherwise, I'd never get laid again.

But nothing compared. Sad, but true. One regrettable night had erased all the work I'd done to get Evan out of my system. The men who'd come after him during my twenties paled in comparison. They might as well have never existed.

It would be better for me to go home rather than drink myself into oblivion in yet another dark, loud club where everyone was having fun except for me. I could curse myself for free in my apartment and wish like hell there was a way to erase the past.

6

EVAN

One thing was painfully obvious as I sat across from Valentina in the country club restaurant.

I needed to get laid.

And soon.

"What's wrong?" She tipped her head to the side, then dabbed the corners of her mouth with a napkin after testing a slice of chateaubriand. "You look like you swallowed something bad."

If only that were my problem.

If only I could take my eyes off her.

If my fucking dick would stop getting uncomfortably thick every time she put something in her mouth. "I'm good," I croaked." Why was my mouth so dry? "Distracted, I guess."

"Please, don't tell me you have bad news," she warned in a flat voice. "I could not take bad news right now."

"Don't worry. Everything's good." Except for the extreme discomfort in my fucking boxer briefs. *Goddammit.* I had yet to get my shit together around her. All she had to do was open her mouth and slide the tines of a fork between her lips, and I was ready to start humping her like a rabid dog. *Did rabid dogs fuck? Jesus Christ, how the fuck did I know?*

I was miserable, not to mention increasingly pissed that I had to behave myself when it was the last thing I wanted to do. It would've been so natural, taking her by the hand and leading her up to my office where we would do things I could not risk thinking about right now. I was uncomfortable enough as it was, fighting a raging hard-on and glad she couldn't see it, thanks to the table between us.

"You've got a hell of a kitchen here." She speared another small bite of succulent beef on the end of her fork. I couldn't breathe as I watched her raise the fork, parting her lips and sliding the meat onto her tongue. She was killing me.

None of this would've been such a problem if I could just get laid. This was the dry spell to end all dry spells, barring the time I broke my collarbone playing a game of basketball. Sex was the furthest thing from my mind then. But that was what it took, some of the worst pain I'd ever experienced to wipe the thought of fucking my brains out. Otherwise, it was never a problem finding a willing woman.

The women weren't the problem. It was me this time. I couldn't muster enough interest in anyone.

That wasn't true, was it?

The problem only got worse when Valentina's eyes closed, and a soft moan stirred in her throat. "God, that is so good," she whispered, chuckling when her eyes opened. "I swear, I should buy a place out here for the excuse to eat every meal in this dining room."

"Wait until you see what the pastry chef can do," I told her, snagging the last bite of beef. "You think this is good? His key lime tarts will melt your panties clean off."

It slipped out before I had a chance to reign in back in.

Goddammit, Evan. What the fuck?

"There you go, thinking about my panties," she murmured, sighing as she made a note on her tablet. I couldn't tell if she hated the idea or what. "Anyway, I think offering the beef or the salmon in dill sauce would be a good move for entrées. We'll need a vegetarian option as well."

"I thought of that." Crooking my fingers, I signaled one of the servers, who brought us a platter of housemade gnocchi in a pear and gorgonzola sauce. "Give this a shot. We could change the sauce if you want, but the gnocchi are second to none."

"I am going to need a week at the gym after all this food." She didn't exactly sound unhappy, though, as she picked up her fork. I had tasted the dish hundreds of times —one of my favorites on the menu. I was perfectly content to sit back and watch her, anticipating her reaction.

She did not disappoint. "Fuck," she groaned out, closing her eyes and taking a deep breath while she chewed slowly. "I have died and gone to heaven. Holy shit."

I couldn't stop staring at the drop of creamy sauce clinging to the corner of her mouth. Hunger unfurled in me, much deeper than a need for food. I needed her here, now. We were two healthy, discreet adults. Why the fuck were we pretending we weren't interested in each other?

Oh, right, because I had fucked up everything, and she was probably too wounded to entertain the idea. On top of that, we were working together. I couldn't afford to forget that either. There were always complications once sex entered the picture.

Like the one I struggled with right now, digging my short nails into my thighs to fight off the impulse to clear the table with a sweep of my arm and make a meal out of her. Now, not only was my cock twitching in anticipation, but my mouth was salivating for a reason that had nothing to do with the food.

It was so damn good when we were together that nobody could blame me for wanting more of her.

"This is absolutely sinful." She moaned before taking another bite of the pillowy ricotta dumplings. "Oh, I could drown in this sauce."

Her eyes opened to find me blatantly staring, hanging onto her every breath, every move she made. At first, I prepared myself to get slapped across the face for staring like I was. At the very least, I figured I would get called out.

Neither of those things happened. Instead, her eyes twinkled wickedly as she slid the tip of her tongue from between her lips and caught the drop of sauce.

Fuck me to tears.

Was she playing with me?

It wouldn't be the first time but so much water had run under the bridge since then. She had never come close to flirting since I walked out on us.

Again.

"Are you going to join me, or would you rather watch me lick up every drop?" She dragged her fork through the sauce, then flicked her tongue over the tines while her gaze never wavered. She was watching me, daring me to react.

I wasn't making it up. She was doing this on purpose, knowing damn well she was driving me wild and testing every ounce of self-control. Valentina hadn't changed, not really. She was still the girl I fell for way back when.

I needed a sip of water to help my dry mouth once she licked the fork clean. "I've always liked watching a woman enjoy herself," I replied, adding a smile, though my boxer briefs were starting to constrict at a painful level.

Her lips twitched like she was trying to suppress a smile. "You don't look like you're enjoying yourself too much."

She was getting off on this, seeing how far she could go before I had to admit defeat. There was only so much a man could stand.

"It's enough that you're having fun." *You evil vixen.* I wasn't allowed to fuck around, flirt with her, acknowledge the tension between us. But she could practically have an orgasm over gnocchi, and it was fine.

"That's nice of you."

What was the game? Why the hell did she insist on keeping me on my toes like this? One minute, we were supposed to forget what happened. The next, she was doing everything short of flashing her tits to get me hard.

I couldn't pretend the exhilaration wasn't appealing, almost addictive. I didn't like feeling I wasn't in on the joke, was all. That was the problem. Having no clue what was going on in that gorgeous head of hers.

"Excuse me. I need to freshen up." She pushed back from the table and stood, leaving me fighting for my life at the sight of the light, sexy sundress she wore. What was it about a sundress that was so damn irresistible? The way it skimmed her legs, the way it hinted at what was underneath. It looked innocent on the surface but could stir up all kinds of thoughts that were anything but.

I pointed her in the direction of the alcove where the restrooms were located, waiting until she disappeared around the corner to lean back in my chair and blow out a deep breath. She hadn't changed her ways, still wild under that worldly veneer. I always assumed she had grown out of it, that she had matured beyond the thrill of getting a guy hard in public.

Like the night we were first together. Half a lifetime ago,

during Colton's high school graduation dinner. I had known her for years by then, the two of us being in the same class, but there had never been anything remotely sexual between us. She was gorgeous and fun to be around, but she might as well have been my sister. Colton was that protective of her and her twin.

Something was different. The air shifted somehow when we sat next to each other at the long table in the back room of an Italian restaurant reserved for this special night. Electricity crackled between us. It didn't matter that I couldn't figure out where it came from or how it started. All I knew was she looked hotter than I had ever seen her, and she kept brushing against me as she reached for the platters of food served family-style.

"Oh, sorry," she murmured, leaning over and rubbing her tits against my arm. No way that was an accident. Still, even though I had nothing to do with it, I looked around, almost paralyzed by guilt. I wasn't part of the family and was honored they would invite me out like this. I didn't want to insult anybody.

"What are you so tense about?" She smelled like vanilla and sugar, sunshine and sunscreen after we had spent the day on the beach behind the Black family's Hampton house. "Come on. Did you think I didn't notice you today?"

"What do you mean?" Right away, my pulse tripled since I knew what she was talking about. I didn't know I was so obvious. But that white bikini she wore barely covered her ass and had me holding my breath the whole day, waiting for the bounce that would send her tits spilling out from the skimpy top.

"You were staring at me the whole afternoon," she whispered, her lips so close to my ear they tickled the lobe. "Don't worry. I didn't mind. It sort of got me wet."

Holy fuck. I looked around again, caught between horror and an instant erection. "Did you sneak something out of the liquor cabinet back at the house?" I asked softly.

She shook her head slowly, a smile playing over her lips. She was the most beautiful thing I had ever seen, not to mention wild, hot, and exciting. "Meet me in back of the restaurant," she whispered. "Don't keep me waiting."

I would be the world's biggest asshole if I turned down an offer like that, but how much was I risking by following orders? Everybody was having a great time, laughing, drinking, and eating. Nobody had been paying us any attention.

What did she have in mind? Was this all a joke?

I only knew one thing. I'd hate myself forever if I didn't at least meet her outside. We didn't have to do anything. I only wanted to know the game she was playing. The humid air hit me like a brick wall when I opened the door and ducked out, pretending I was going to the bathroom. It was dark, a single bulb over the door giving me barely enough light to see. There wasn't much to admire besides a pair of dumpsters.

If this was all a prank to lock me out of the restaurant or some dumb shit like that...

"Over here." Valentina leaned out from the other side of the dumpsters, beckoning me with a hand. "I won't bite."

My legs were shaking, and my dick was ready to tear through my khaki pants, but I followed orders, meeting her in the darkness. "What the fuck is going on?" I whispered, slapping at a mosquito on my arm. This needed to be worth it.

She didn't answer in words. The hand gripping the back of my neck and pulling me down for a deep kiss said everything.

The memory was enough to get out of my chair. We weren't kids anymore, and I wasn't going to wait around for her to decide game time was over. I marched across the dining room, quiet in the late morning before customers came in for lunch, and stepped into the alcove hidden from the rest of the room only a moment before she opened the bathroom door to find me waiting.

This time, I was the one pushing her against the wall, plunging my tongue into her mouth. The tangy taste of gorgonzola lingered, but it was her needy grunts that stole my focus. She reached up, fingers tugging at my hair, her tongue stroking mine until I was sure I would go insane from the need to be inside her.

She gasped at the touch of my hand against her thigh, sliding under her dress to cup her tight ass cheek. Lifting a leg and hooking it around my hip, she drew me closer, locking me in place. There was nowhere I'd rather be than here, tangled up in her, my heart pounding out of my chest and my dick threatening to break my zipper.

I hissed when she sucked my bottom lip, biting down almost hard enough to break the skin, but all the added sensation did was make me crave her more. My blood was on fire, my dick dripping and waiting to be put to use. I molded one of her tits in my hand, testing its weight, running my thumb over the nub jutting out from under her bra and dress. How could I have passed up the opportunity to have her like this all the time? So hot, writhing, and perfect.

"Evan..." she whispered when I broke the kiss to taste the skin of her throat while she clawed at my shoulders. "Oh, God..."

I would make her see God before this was over. Fuck acting like we could keep this professional. Now that we had opened that rusted old door between the past and the present, there was no shutting it again. No pretending. "You thought I'd let you get away with it?" I grunted, grinding against her, making her whimper. "Getting me hard like this? You need to be punished."

"Punish me," she begged, meeting my mouth again, our teeth clashing as we fought for control.

"Mr. Anderson?" A soft female voice floated our way from the dining room. For one wild moment, I considered ignoring it, pretending I hadn't heard. I wasn't going to let an employee end this when I finally had Valentina where I wanted her.

Unfortunately, she had sharp hearing too. "Shit." The hands that just seconds ago were clawing my shoulders now pushed them away. "Dammit, this is all wrong. We can't do this."

It was more than an uncomfortable hard-on that made me grind my teeth. "What the fuck?" I growled, breathless, needy, and fucking annoyed at the way she immediately changed her mind. "What is it? One minute, you're turning a taste test into a porno with all that moaning and shit, and the next minute you're telling me it's a mistake? Make up your fucking mind," I spat.

"You're right." She fixed her dress, making sure her tits were covered, then smoothed a few strands of hair behind her ears. "That was my mistake. I was screwing around back there, teasing you. It won't happen again."

"Bullshit," I fired back. "You've already said that, remember?"

Her eyes narrowed to slits. "Maybe I needed to be reminded why this is a bad idea. So thanks for the reminder."

"What is that supposed to mean?"

"It means I keep forgetting who you are because you're good with your hands and your dick." There was so much bitterness in the way she said it, dripping from every word, that I was stunned into silence.

I couldn't come up with anything to say before she left, her sandals slapping the floor with every quick step. She wasn't going back to the table. She was leaving the country club, which was for the best, considering how tempting it was to tell her to go fuck herself if she thought I was some-body she could play with. If she wanted to punish me for my childish choices, that was one thing. I would've respected her more if she would come out and say it instead of screwing with my head.

Instead, I did the only thing I could do to get through the rest of my day. "One minute," I called out to the faceless employee who had interrupted us.

Ducking into the men's room, I stepped into the first stall and closed the door before lowering my zipper and freeing my erect dick. I closed my eyes and leaned against the stall door, wrapping my fist around my shaft and working it quickly, desperately, already so close to the edge. I could still taste her, and I focused on that, the memory of her moans, the way her light, floral scent clung to my suit jacket. All of it worked on me, pushing me, making my heart pound and my balls lift.

I was barely able to grab a wad of toilet paper before I exploded, my ears ringing from the force of one spurt after another. "Valentina," I whispered once it was over, tipping my head back against the wall and heaving a sigh.

There was no way I would make it through the next five weeks this way. Something had to change. The problem was, I had no idea what or how I'd change it when I was this weak for her.

7

VALENTINA

"**C**ome on, you guys..." This was the third time I tried to steer the conversation back toward the purpose of everybody gathering at my apartment. I would've had a better chance of herding cats. Nobody wanted to focus, and my jaw ached from clenching it so tight. "I'm only trying to firm up the list of ideas so we can put an itinerary together for the wedding weekend. The sooner we finish, the sooner you can all enjoy your Friday night."

Yet, throughout the calamity of it all, my mind still went *there*. With him, fooling around, then getting caught. Wishing we hadn't.

"Everybody listen to her," Rose's voice cut through my heated thoughts, and my gaze darted to hers, where she rested her legs in Colton's lap. Like him, she had come straight from work, and now her heels sat on the floor while he rubbed her feet. "Otherwise, don't complain when you end up having to do something you don't want to do before the wedding."

"I mean, I thought we had things pretty much settled."

Lucian tossed an olive in the air and caught it in his mouth, earning faint applause from the rest of the group. "Golfing and sailing on Saturday, wedding on Sunday. I guess we'll have a rehearsal dinner?" he asked, looking around. Clearly, he was in a hurry to move on with the evening.

"Of course," Colton confirmed. "At the country club, right?" he asked Evan, who nodded.

He had been ominously silent since showing up an hour ago. That was fine with me. The less he said, the sooner we could get this over with, and he could leave. I was too annoyed with him and with myself after Wednesday's fiasco to face him. What a shame I had no choice.

You had a choice not to screw with him. Right, but I couldn't resist. Who could? Sitting there, watching him turn into some throbbing, aching pile of horniness. He hadn't tried to hide it, openly ogling me with his tongue practically hanging out of his mouth.

I never could turn down the chance to make a man squirm, especially when that man happened to be some-body who broke my heart—any little way I could get a piece of my pride back.

Okay, so it was fun too. But then he went and kissed me, and everything flipped around. Now I was the one who wished I hadn't been such a horny, needy mess who had basically humped him in the middle of his place of business. I knew better than that.

"What about the Friday before?" I prompted. "The spa at the Delamar looks amazing. I've already booked a group package for the Friday before the wedding. Massages, facials, mani-pedi. A whole day of pampering. What about the guys, though?" I asked, looking around for ideas.

Evan gave me nothing, blank-faced. Was he sulking now?

"Any good strip clubs in the area?" Lucian suggested, earning dirty looks from all of the girls, including me.

"We're thinking something a little more family-friendly," I pointed out, rolling my eyes. "Besides, the answer's probably no anyway."

"Not that I'm interested in doing that," Colton insisted, even though nobody asked. "I never cared about strip clubs anyway. It's all an act."

"If I want somebody to strip for me..." Noah grabbed Sienna, who giggled while he pulled her into his lap. "I'm all set. I don't need to pay for it."

Why the hell did it make my heart hurt to see them so happy? I was turning into a complete disaster over this wedding and everything around it.

"How about a fishing trip?" Evan suggested. "We could take a yacht out from the harbor. The hotel is right there and spend the afternoon on the water."

"So long as this one promises to wear sunscreen." Rose nudged Colton. "I don't want you sunburned for our photos."

"Same goes for you," he retorted. "I'm not trying to marry a lobster in a wedding gown."

"How romantic." Aria snickered, rolling her eyes as she walked past them with a glass of wine in hand. Rose looked so envious, and I felt sorry for her.

"Aria here will make certain the girls are slathered in sunscreen," he offered.

We threw around another few ideas, including the shopping trip on Greenwich Avenue and a group excursion to the Audubon Center to explore the nature trails. "And we're good on rehearsal plans?" I asked, looking at Colton, who insisted on being my point person. "You're okay with the menu, the schedule?"

"This is completely in your hands. I trust you." When I continued to stare daggers at him, he nodded. "Sure. Everything's great. No suggestions."

"Thank you." Trust was nice, but verbal confirmation was more important.

"What do we do now?" Noah threw his arms overhead, stretching as we wrapped things up. "Wanna go out for drinks?"

"We're drinking here," Aria pointed out, lifting her wine glass.

"You know what I mean," he grumbled. "Do we want to go out?"

"I'm really not feeling up to it," Rose admitted, looking around like she felt guilty. "Sorry."

"There's nothing to apologize for. Besides..." Sienna offered, "... I'm not feeling it either. I think I just want to take a bath and put on a mask. But you boys are more than welcome to do whatever," she added, offering her boyfriend an apologetic smile.

"Ah, fuck it," Noah decided. "I have a couple of contracts to look over anyway."

Poor Lucian. He looked around like a puppy whose favorite toy had been taken away. "Seriously? Evan?"

Evan shrugged a shoulder. Until now, he may as well have been a statue sitting in my armchair. Tapping his fingers against his knee, he shook his head. "I have to go out to the Cape Cod location first thing in the morning. We're having some work done to the clubhouse," he explained with a sigh.

"You know, there's a reason you pay people to work for you," Colton reminded him. "So they can be the ones to do the shit work like driving out to Cape Cod first thing in the morning. On a Saturday, at that."

Evan only scowled. "I don't trust anybody as much as I trust myself."

Aria laughed. "You sound like somebody I know." She turned to me. "Practically begging for burnout."

"I'm a hands-on girl," I explained.

Unfortunately, all I could think about was getting my hands on Evan. As annoyed as I was, as embarrassed after my shameful performance earlier this week, I couldn't take my eyes off him. Why did he have to be... him, looking like walking sin in a striped shirt with its top two buttons popped open and a pair of pants whose seams were extremely strong, considering they held fast around those thick thighs of his?

It was my turn to stare at him like some deranged psycho tonight, it seemed.

Lucian dragged his feet out of my apartment. "Sure you don't wanna go have some fun?" he asked me.

"I'm beat," I told him, and I wasn't lying. I was downright exhausted, and there were still a bunch of emails I needed to follow up on. "You'll have to have a little fun on your own. But we both know you won't be on your own for long." That got him laughing as he headed out.

Noah and Sienna followed him, with Sienna confirming availability for dress fittings in a couple of weeks.

"See you later." Evan slung his suit jacket over one arm, barely looking my way before joining Colton and Rose on their way out.

Aria and Miles brought up the rear, with Aria stopping to hug me. "Try to get some rest," she urged, studying me while Miles waited for her by the elevator. "You look exhausted."

"And you are going to give me a complex about myself," I retorted before playfully shoving her out into the hall. "If

I end up with a face full of filler before I'm thirty, it's on you."

At least it was something to laugh about as I closed and locked the door, leaving me on my own. The loft was almost painfully quiet after being filled with laughter and voices a couple of minutes ago.

I valued my solitude above most things. This was my safe place, my refuge, but there was a thin line between that and loneliness. I didn't know that line existed until now as I wandered around, picking up glasses and tossing what little was left of the snacks I'd put out. Most of them had someone to go home to. Somebody to be with. I had emails, a vibrator, and what was left of the wine.

A sudden, hard knock at the door startled me into almost dropping a wine glass on the floor. "Lucian, I meant it," I muttered on my way across the living room. "I'm not in the mood." I wouldn't have put it past him to try to convince me to come out, after all.

So, I was in no way prepared to find Evan standing in front of me when I swung the door open. "I left my tie," he explained. "It's probably on the chair."

Dammit. He had a way of knocking me off balance. "Go ahead," I shrugged, stepping aside so he could enter. He was so overwhelming in every way—his size, not to mention that damn cologne he insisted on wearing. Something he must have worn in the years since we broke up, right? Why had it never mattered as much as it did now when it turned my knees to jelly?

"You know," I told him, turning to watch him fish for his tie in the space between the arm of the chair and the cushion. "I could have brought you the tie whenever you wanted. You didn't need to come back up for it."

"I figured I was still downstairs and might as well grab

it." He pulled out a length of navy blue silk and folded it neatly before tucking it inside his jacket pocket.

"Are you sure that wasn't just an excuse to come back up here?" And it was. Time might have passed, but I could still see through him. Just like I could when I was sampling those dishes at his country club. He might as well have written his thoughts across his high forehead.

"Do you ever get tired of busting balls?" He tossed his jacket over the back of the chair before his brows knitted together. "I wanted to clear things up after Wednesday. I shouldn't have thrown all that shit at you when I jumped you like that."

For once, we were clearing the air after an argument. Did this qualify as growth? "It's not your fault. I was messing with you, which you know," I admitted when he scowled. "You were right to call me out. I don't know why I wanted so much to tease you the way I did."

That was all it took. One little admission.

The air in the room shifted until it crackled with energy. "I know why," he told me in a low voice full of danger, taking one slow step after another in my direction.

Red flags waved in my head. "Wait a second."

Either he didn't hear me, or he didn't care. "Why don't you make up your mind?" he asked, stalking me like he was the hunter and I was the prey. I couldn't deny the heat racing its way up my spine, making my breath come shorter and ragged. "Either you want me, or you don't. And we both know you do. Why are you hell-bent on pretending otherwise?"

There was a plain answer to that question, but I didn't want to get into it. Not now, not when the sight of his lustful stare stirred unspeakable heat in my core.

No, this couldn't happen. If I didn't trust him with the

truth, how could I trust him with my body? *Because he's so damn good at it.*

Feelings and sex didn't have to go hand in hand. The best sex was usually with the person it would be the worst idea to get serious with.

Just this one more time.

What would it hurt?

I knew before he reached me it was always going to be this way. We couldn't be in the same room anymore without this explosion of heat, the sort that made a girl want to take her clothes off. I was wet by the time he ran the backs of his fingers down my cheek, my body already prepared and hungry for what I knew he would give me. Escape. Release. I didn't know how much I craved them until now when his touch promised so much. No way would I risk losing it by telling him exactly why we were probably making a mistake by doing this.

"Not upstairs," I whispered, taking him by the hand and pulling him to the chair he sat in earlier and probably hid his tie in so he'd have a reason to come back.

Dropping his pants and black boxer shorts, I shoved him down and then straddled him. If we were going to do this, it would happen my way.

I pulled the foil wrapper from his grasp and tore it open with my teeth before rolling it along his swollen cock.

"What are you doing to me?" he hissed in the instant before we kissed.

He thought I was doing something to him? He was the one making me doubt everything I ever thought I knew, wanted, or believed about myself. He made me throw everything I remembered out the window in favor of scratching an itch only he could reach.

I couldn't think about that now, not once I impaled

myself on his rigid cock. Sheer, open-mouthed pleasure washed over me and demanded I ride him for all I was worth, to forget everything, to let it all go. It didn't have to mean anything but a good time. I wouldn't let it.

It was getting easier to lie to myself.

8

EVAN

"Mr. Black, you didn't have to do this." My stomach was about to burst by the time I finished the enormous meal we had put away between the three of us. The remnants were scattered across plates in the center of the table.

"And you don't have to call me Mr. Black," Barrett reminded me with a fatherly grin. "I thought we were on a first-name basis by now."

Some lessons were impossible to shake after being drilled into a guy's brain his entire childhood, even after fifteen years of acquaintance. "Okay, *Barrett*." I chuckled. "Thank you for dinner."

"It was my pleasure." His cheeks puffed when he blew out a sigh. "I don't know why I thought I could put that much food away. I used to be able to, back when I was your age. The two of you make me feel young again. I'll blame my indigestion overnight on you."

We laughed along with Colton, who refilled our glasses with the same rich merlot we'd enjoyed throughout the meal. "I've been blamed for a lot worse than that," he muttered, smirking at his father when their eyes met. Only faint wrinkles and graying hair set Barrett apart from his son. It was almost freaky how well he'd aged.

"Water under the bridge, son. At least, that's what I hope." Barrett slid me an apologetic glance. "Evan here didn't come out to listen to us rehashing the past."

"If anything," Colton continued. "It's been a little unnerving. You haven't criticized me nearly enough in the past few months. Not even for getting my girlfriend pregnant."

This was taking an interesting turn. I was unfamiliar with this level of honesty between a father and son. It wasn't that I had a bad relationship with my parents. More like a distant one. Surface-level shit, nothing deeper than that.

It was the way Dad was raised by his emotionally crippled father, and the cycle continued. It would end with me since the chances of my settling down and starting a family were minuscule. Not all of us were lucky like Colton, with loving parents who hadn't left him alone to basically raise himself the way mine had. I wouldn't know the first thing about being a decent husband or father and couldn't see putting anybody through living with me, no matter how happy my friends seemed now that they were settling down.

Another foreign thing. The pang in my chest at that thought, and the discomfort and disappointment.

The image of Valentina that filled my memory. She had been on my mind lately, and it made sense she'd show up in my mind's eye now. There would always be what could have been.

Everything worked out for the best.

I still believed that.

"Rose has been a good influence on you," Barrett pointed out, swirling the wine in his wide glass. "You're a changed man. Finally living up to your potential. Settling down, starting a family, that's a good thing. It makes your mother and I very happy to see you stepping into this next phase of your life."

He then turned to me, raising his glass. "And you're making the wedding possible. Nothing like short notice, right?"

"It's a pleasure." And it had been in more ways than one.

Part of my attention was always on Valentina, meaning my dick twitched in my pants when I remembered just how much of a pleasure the past few weeks had been. She drove me crazy and invaded my concentration time and again, but the payoff? More than worth it every time we were together.

"When will it be your turn, do you think?" When I blurted out a laugh at the sudden question, Barrett lifted a hand and shook his head. "Sorry, I've spent too many years married to my wife. I'm starting to think like her. But you're practically a member of the family. That gives me the right to ask an uncomfortable question every couple of years or so."

Colton's mouth twitched like he was trying not to grin. "Yeah, Evan. When *will* it be your turn?" he taunted, leaning back in his chair with his eyes crinkling at the corners the way they did when he busted my balls.

"I've yet to find a woman who can handle me." I sighed, making them both laugh. Good. Let them laugh. Humor was my fallback, getting me out of a sticky situation once again.

Though not for long.

"You have to stay open to the possibility. I know, I sound like some dating advice column." Barrett ran a hand over the back of his neck, squinting. "Do they still have those?"

"I have no idea," I admitted. "I've never looked for advice with women."

"Anyway, it's good advice," he insisted. "Enjoy being young and single, definitely. I sure as hell did." That came as no surprise.

We all knew stories of the stuff he and his friends got into when they were our age. The hunk holes, they were called, partying and fucking their way through Manhattan without giving a damn. Years spent with the family left me with plenty of stories and legends overheard during get-togethers.

"No problem there," I assured him, chuckling and sipping my wine. This turn of conversation had me feeling pretty fucking uncomfortable, but I couldn't be rude to a man who, at times, seemed more like my father than my own ever had.

I never understood the contention between Barrett and Colton all those years—at least, not when I looked at it from my point of view. Barrett was hard on him, but at least he gave a shit.

"Years from now..." Barrett continued, "... the partying and the women and the freedom... it will get stale. Trust me on that. No party can last forever. I couldn't have imagined it at your age, but the satisfaction I got from being a father and a husband? No amount of anonymous sex could top that."

"Nice, Dad," Colton muttered, snickering. "Hang on. Let me grab my notebook and jot this down."

"Be a smartass all you want," Barrett retorted. "You know I'm right. Or are you not happier now than you were before you and Rose got together?"

Colton rolled his eyes, grumbling. He didn't like being backed into a corner, which his father had successfully done. "Fine, whatever you say. You're right. But I'm not going to be that asshole who finds a woman and decides everybody he knows needs to commit the way he has."

"Fair enough." Barrett gave me a wink. "For now, you can be satisfied knowing you're making Rose extremely happy. The rest of us too. I know it can't be easy, putting something like this together at the last minute."

"You can thank Valentina for a lot of that." Speaking her name had a weird effect on me. My heart swelled, and a warm, peaceful feeling settled over me. "She's bent over backward, called in every favor she's owed to make this work. I swear, I don't know when she sleeps."

"Well, we always did know she's the ultimate Type A personality," Colton pointed out. "We couldn't have a play-date when we were kids without her trying to set an itinerary."

I could easily imagine that. "She's driven," I agreed.

"Like her mom," Barrett suggested with a fond smile. One thing was never in doubt. He adored his sister, Evelyn. "Once she gets something in her head, you can't change her mind."

Like the idea I would hurt her again.

Like the idea I was some heartless fuck who couldn't be trusted.

Once Barrett settled the check, I shook his hand and thanked him again for the dinner. "It was a pleasure," he assured me. "Now, I expect you'll head out to see who you can find tonight?"

Normally, I would have. Countless clubs and bars to choose from. Countless women too. The problem was, only one woman held any interest since the fateful night I sunk my dick in her again.

"Something like that."

I promised Colton a phone call soon before setting off

on foot from the restaurant. Somebody happened to live only a few blocks away. The only person I wanted to see tonight. There was no way I'd get a minute's sleep without seeing her and doing a lot more than that.

Valentina was close to the top of my list of text message threads. I pulled her up and sent a message while strolling down Thirty-Fourth Street in the direction of her building.

Me: *Where are you? It's important.*

If she wasn't at home, I would find her. It was starting to become a quest. Something I had to do before my head hit the pillow.

My phone buzzed, and I couldn't remember the last time my heart leaped at a new text message. She was turning me into somebody I swore I'd never be. At the moment, anticipating her response, I couldn't be bothered to care.

Valentina: *At home, but not for long. Why?*

Me: *Need to meet you there ASAP.*

The foot traffic and passing cars meant nothing. I barely noticed them. She was home, and I was beyond sick and tired of pretending it was possible to ignore the permanent hard-on I had for her.

Valentina: *Can it wait until tomorrow? I'm in the middle of something.*

Like what? Getting ready to go out so some asshole could try his luck? That wasn't going to happen.

Me: *What's so important?*

Valentina: *I just got out of the shower, if you need to know.*

What an image.

Me: *It's an emergency. I have to see you. Tonight.*

She didn't keep me waiting long, offering a short reply.

Valentina: *Fine.*

Me: *Good, because I'm outside your building. Be right up.*

I chuckled to myself, imagining her reaction while the

elevator crawled up to her floor. Now that I knew what I wanted, I couldn't wait another minute to have her. She wanted me too. That was obvious. Time to stop acting like there was anything we could do about it.

Her front door opened within moments of my fist striking the wood. Her hair was in a bun, wet strands hanging around her fresh, shining face. The tank and shorts she wore clung to her damp skin. "Well?" she demanded, tits heaving like she had run down the stairs.

Desire stole my voice before I stepped over the threshold. The floral scent of her body wash hung in the air, wrapping me in a cloud of sensory input I couldn't begin to process when lust took up so much of my brain.

"What's so important?" She was wide-eyed, standing with her hands on her hips and her shoulders pulled up around her ears. "Please, tell me there's not a conflict or cancellation. I don't think my nerves could stand it."

I had a bigger problem on my hands. Like the fact I couldn't stand much more of being this close to her without putting my hands on her. I closed and locked the door, my heart pounding with determination.

She threw her hands into the air. "Hello, asshole! I barely had a chance to dry off after my shower because you said it was an emergency. What is it, already?"

I wanted to find the words. I did. A way to tell her I was sorry for what happened, the way it happened. To tell her I wanted to start over again. We couldn't pick up where we left off, but we could start fresh if she would let us. I didn't need a commitment. I only needed right now, this moment, and I would have said anything to make that happen.

Except, I couldn't find the words. I had no practice apologizing and even less when it came to explaining my feelings. What I needed.

The next best thing was taking her by the waist and pushing her up against the door before holding her there with my body. "This," I whispered before my self-control shattered, and I covered her mouth with mine. It was always like this, the rush of claiming her. The sense of coming home, where I belonged, where I never should have left.

She indulged me for a few heart-stopping seconds before turning her head sharply to break the kiss. "What the hell do you think you're doing?" she whispered, her chest heaving, eyes burning when they found mine. "You don't get to drag me over here for a booty call. You don't have booty call privileges."

"Are you sure about that?" Trailing a hand down her side, I could barely contain the shiver of anticipation that ran through me when her breath caught, her back arching and pressing her tits against my chest. "Because you don't seem to mind this."

"My body might not, but my brain is another story." Her nostrils flared over clenched teeth which she bared at me in a snarl.

I couldn't lose this. Not when I had her here, so close. "Tell your brain to shut the fuck up," I suggested, grinning when she rolled her eyes. "I don't know about you, but I cannot spend the next four weeks pretending I don't want you. You know I do. Not a day goes by that I don't wish I could be inside you."

"Evan..." she whispered the way a person did when resistance was fading. She was getting weak, but then she had never been that strong to begin with. She only wanted to believe she was.

"And that's going to keep going as long as we work together." My already hard cock turned to steel when I dug my fingers into her ass. "Why are we wasting time fighting this?"

"Because..." Her tongue darted over her lips to moisten them, and the sight made me groan. That was what she did to me. All it took was a simple gesture, and I was hooked.

"You can't come up with a reason, can you?" I dragged my thumb across her full bottom lip, and she sighed, eyes sliding shut, her breath hot on my skin. "Why bother trying? I'm not going to bother trying to pretend I don't want you."

My lips replaced my thumb, brushing softly over her mouth, leaving her whimpering. She was as helpless against this as I was. Heat raced through my veins, compelling me to do it again, to make her melt against me, to make her part her lips and touch her tongue to mine. I had never been this hard, this desperate to sink in deep and fuck her until she forgot every reservation she ever had.

"God, why are we doing this?" She gazed up at me, looking dazed and hungry. "Why am I letting you do this to me?"

That much I knew beyond a doubt. "Because it is so fucking good when I do," I reminded her, grinning at the understanding in her gaze before kissing her again.

This time, she didn't stop me.

9

VALENTINA

Traffic was light on my way to the bakery to test cake flavors. We had four weeks to go, and I had never felt so much like I was behind the controls of a speeding train whose brakes were gone.

"Did you get the updated list of RSVPs together?" I asked Bianca as I turned onto Greenwich Street.

"Sure did, and I forwarded it to you." Bianca was breathless and overwhelmed, as always. I'd have to encourage her to take a vacation when this was over.

"Great. I need to work on the seating arrangements over the weekend." A couple of kids crossed in the middle of the street without looking, making me slam on the brakes and tap my horn to get their attention. They were maybe nine, ten years old.

The age my child would've been.A lump formed in my throat as a tsunami of sadness washed over me.

The driver behind me sounded their horn, pulling me out of my despair, but not before I stuck a hand out the window and flipped them off. "I'll stop by the florist after the cake tasting to make sure they have enough hands on

deck when it comes time to start putting things together."
A side project like the one I had given them would take a
lot of extra effort on top of the arrangements for the
wedding. I was paying for it out of my pocket, my gift to
Rose. She would absolutely love it if we managed to pull
it off.

"Are you sure you're going to have time? They're talking
about a big storm coming in this afternoon."

The sky was pretty ominous. "Are they? Wow, I'm
usually on top of things like this." I usually wasn't sleep
deprived, but three straight nights of fucking like the world
was coming to an end wasn't something I was used to either.

With Evan, no less.

Mixed feelings made my stomach churn, but I brushed
the sensation aside. We were adults. I had needs. It just so
happened a decade of experience made him an expert at
satisfying them. I wouldn't have known that if it wasn't for a
night of weakness, and now I couldn't forget. We'd get it out
of our systems and move on once the wedding was over.

We had to. *Right?* It's not like there was a plausible
alternative.

Bianca was blissfully unaware of my rationalization, still
fretting. "You don't want to get caught in it. Maybe it would
be better to postpone the florist until tomorrow."

"I'll be fine," I insisted, parking in the lot along the rear
of a string of businesses. "It won't take long at the bakery,
and I can always use the storm as an excuse to cut out if
things start running over schedule."

"Just to be safe out there," she urged. I promised I would,
then ended the call and stepped out of the car. The air was
suspiciously humid, especially for early May when it didn't
usually feel like this. An upward glance served as a
reminder of what was coming—dark clouds rolling fast, and

it was definitely windier than it was when I set out for Greenwich earlier.

All the more reason to get the hell in there and get this over with.

It wasn't the promise of a storm that made my heart race as I stepped into the quaint, cheerful little shop. Like many businesses in this part of town, the historic building was full of charm and stunning architectural details. The owners had leaned into it, creating a vibe I could only describe as old-timey. Like stepping back a century, though I doubted items like cake pops and cronuts existed back then.

I had never spoken to the head baker. Until now, Evan had been in charge of that. I hated giving up even a tiny bit of control, but desperate times called for desperate measures. There were only so many hours in the day, only so many phone calls I could possibly make.

I only knew her name, so the sight of Marissa written across the name tag of the girl who stepped through swinging doors made me extend a hand over the counter. "I'm Valentina Miller, here for a cake tasting for the Goldsmith-Black wedding next month."

She rubbed a hand across the front of her apron, leaving a smudge of flour before shaking. "Nice to meet you. Everything's all set up in back. Follow me."

"Is Mr. Anderson here yet?" I couldn't be annoyed at him for wanting to be part of the cake tasting the way I would've been before he somehow managed to break down my defenses at my apartment. If anything, there was a tiny thrill in pretending there was nothing going on between us. I'd forgotten how much fun it could be, having a secret like this.

We were both adults. This had nothing to do with the past, and there was certainly no future in it. It was for now. Fun for now.

"He's waiting for us. Follow me." She flipped up a hinged portion of the front counter, and I followed her into the kitchen.

My heart skipped a beat when I found him sitting at a stainless steel prep table at the far end of the busy kitchen with his shirtsleeves rolled up like he was ready to dig in. In front of him was a row of plates, each holding a different cake flavor, but I was more interested in the man who looked much more delicious than cake ever could.

"Good thing you got here when you did," he warned with a grin as we approached. "I'm not sure I could be a good boy much longer."

The comment was directed my way. At least, it seemed like it was. For some reason, though, Marissa giggled. "Nobody can be a good boy all the time," she reasoned.

Oh. So it was like that. I rolled my shoulders back, staring at the blonde ponytail that swung back and forth in front of me as we approached the stool where Evan sat.

"Sorry to keep you waiting," I offered, pulling out my tablet to take notes on the different flavors with one eye on the flirtatious little baker. She stood across from where I sat next to Evan, leaning in with her elbows on the table and giving him the sort of smile that hinted at a past. Did they have a past? *What the hell do I care anyway?*

No, Evan didn't do that. It wasn't totally outside the realm of possibility that he would sleep with a vendor he frequently did business with, but he didn't like complications. Fuck buddies presented complications. Weren't we a perfect example of that? But I was supposed to be special.

We were... once upon a time.

Was I actually getting jealous over this girl?

"Here we are. The five flavors the bride narrowed down." Marissa gestured at each as she described them. "Champagne-infused sponge with a strawberry frosting. Chocolate sponge with a black cherry filling and mocha frosting. Vanilla bean with raspberry filling and cream cheese frosting with a touch of raspberry purée whipped in. A traditional red velvet with plain cream cheese frosting. Finally, a lemon-infused sponge with blueberry filling and a lemon frosting."

"I think I gained five pounds just listening to all of that," I confessed. Evan chuckled, but Marissa didn't seem to find it funny. She only held out a pair of forks, one for each of us.

Evan turned my way, his brows lifted. He didn't seem to notice the difference between the way she treated him and her standoffish attitude toward me. "Where do you want to start?" he asked with a playful grin that might have melted my panties under different circumstances.

Whenever I forgot why I kept stabbing myself in the back by sleeping with the man who broke my heart, he had to go and do something like that to remind me. The handsome prick.

Where did I want to start? With the faint handprint on his gray jacket. The sort of thing that would get left behind if someone had flour on their hand and touched somebody's chest. I brushed it off with nothing more than a pointed look, but I was definitely going to bring it up later. "Let's start at the beginning. Champagne and strawberry."

"It's one of my favorites," Marissa told us. Like anybody asked. Obviously, she was interested in him, staring as he sank his fork into the slice. Hell, she reminded me of the way he watched me eat back at the country club.

"How do you get it so light?" he asked, chewing slowly. I took a bite for the sake of playing along. It was nice, even if it kind of tasted like sawdust. That had to be a me problem since he was loving it.

"A trick of the trade. I could tell you, but I would have to kill you," she teased. They shared a grin, and I cleared my throat before pushing the plate aside.

"One down," I said, making a note in my app. "That was very nice. Champagne and strawberry, great combination." Not exactly revolutionary.

We tried the chocolate cake next, which had a nice, rich flavor. "I love the cherry with the chocolate," I told Evan, who nodded in agreement before taking a second bite.

"The cherries are a little tart, but it goes well with the sugary frosting," he agreed.

Marissa smiled wide like she'd invented the combination. "A little tartness brings out the sweetness," she explained, dragging her finger through a bit of frosting left on the plate and popping it into her mouth. Oh, boy. She wasn't even trying to hide how blatantly she flirted with him. Sure, he had a great dick and did things with his hands and tongue that were downright magical but come on. She was supposed to be a professional.

Then again, so was I. So was Evan. That didn't stop us from fucking like rabbits whenever we were in the same room for too long.

The lights flickered, making us all look up in unison at the fluorescents overhead. "Looks like that storm is coming in." Marissa went to the back door and opened it, letting in the roar of increasing winds.

It had gotten darker since I came in. "Maybe we should hurry this up," I suggested in a soft voice, and Evan grunted his agreement. Maybe Mother Nature was on my side. The less time I spent with this girl drooling over him, the safer it would be. Otherwise, she might end up with a fistful of hair yanked from her scalp. He wasn't mine. He hadn't been for a long time, but that didn't stop me from seething like a jealous girlfriend.

"I'll have to postpone my trip to the florist," I announced, setting my fork down to send Bianca a text letting her know. She'd be relieved.

"It might be a little late to consider driving home now," he suggested as Marissa joined us again. "I walked over from the club, and I have the house out here. I'd have asked you for a ride home anyway," he joked, winking.

Marissa slid the next cake in front of us. "Vanilla bean." So she didn't like us talking about going back to his place after this. I bit my lip to hide a smile while cutting a piece away. It was good, but not great. My favorite part about it was the bit of frosting left on Evan's chin, which I reached out to brush away.

Not because of the frosting, but because of Miss Handsy, who liked to leave handprints on people who didn't belong to her. Not that he belonged to me.

By the time we tasted the last—and maybe best—cake, the wind gusted hard enough for us to hear it inside the kitchen. "This is phenomenal," Evan assured Marissa as we both stood, collecting ourselves. "But we'd better get going. I hope the roads are still clear."

Marissa's face fell. "Oh, okay. Let me know what you decide." I caught her scowling at me before she could wipe the look off her face. *Sorry, babe, but he's leaving with me.* We said our goodbyes and offered our thanks before ducking out the back door. A few stray raindrops hit the top of my head, but so far, the biggest problem was the roaring wind and thunder rumbling ominously in the distance.

"I'll drop you off at home or take you back to the club. Whatever you want." I unlocked the doors and was happy to escape inside the car, where there was nothing blowing in my face.

"I think it's better if we go home," he decided in a serious voice once he joined me in the passenger seat.

I snorted. "I have work to do. A lot of it. Including taking the RSVPs and arranging the seating based off of who's responded so far. We're talking about a few hundred people."

"No problem. I'll help you with it. That will make it easier."

Damn him. I hated it when he made sense. Who were we kidding, though? We wouldn't get any work done. I couldn't stop staring at his mouth and his hands, remembering what they did to me. "I'd be more productive at home, I think. No offense."

"Don't be ridiculous. It's storming like crazy. You could end up in trouble on the road." He hadn't finished the sentence before big, fat raindrops started to fall. It wasn't the sort of thing where the rain started off slowly and gradually increased. We went from no rain to a downpour in roughly three seconds flat. Soon, the sound filled the inside of the car. It was so loud Evan had to raise his voice. "No way you're driving back to the city in this."

"It's not going to be this way forever," I pointed out.

The smartass had to go and pull out his phone. Opening a weather app, he pulled up the current radar. We were smack dab in the middle of an enormous storm cell, completely covered, and the hourly outlook called for heavy rain and high winds until late evening.

He looked at me.

I looked at him.

"I'm five minutes away from here," he reminded me.

"And I can help you with those seating arrangements if you want."

"Don't act like you want me to come over just to work on the wedding," I warned. It was impossible to keep a straight face when he wore that charming, sexy little grin.

How did he do it? And how the hell did I keep falling for it?

"Fine. Tell me how to get there." I pulled out of the spot and rolled slowly through the lot. Thankfully, there weren't a lot of cars on the street, but I knew that would have changed if I tried to leave town. It was smarter and safer to stay local until the storm passed.

However, I had a hard time believing anything related to an evening alone with Evan could be described as safe.

10

EVAN

By the time we reached the porch wrapping around the first floor of the house, the short run from the car left us soaked. "Holy shit!" Valentina shouted over the rain and thunder, caught between laughter and irritation as she shook out her hair now that we were sheltered from the downpour. "I just hope the weather isn't like this for the—"

"Don't say it," I warned before she could get the words out, pressing buttons on the keypad to unlock the front door. "Let's not jinx ourselves."

"I didn't know you were superstitious."

"I'm not. But let's not invite trouble." Everything surrounding the wedding was going smoothly. Almost too smoothly. I couldn't help but wait for the other shoe to drop the way it did whenever something good came along. I wasn't taking any chances.

I ushered her inside and closed the door on the storm, taking it from deafening to a dull roar in an instant. The lack of sunlight left me flipping a light switch, and Valentina whistled in appreciation as she took it all in. "This is really beautiful," she announced, walking slowly through the entry hall, gazing up the stairs, and turning around in a slow circle. "How long have you had this house?"

"I've lost track of time. A couple years? It made more sense than camping out on a couch in my office or getting a hotel room every time I worked late."

"What kind of square footage are we talking here?" she asked, admiring the ornately carved banister alongside the stairs.

I loved the way her mind worked. "Around twenty-five hundred. And right now, you're too wet to sit on any of my furniture," I pointed out, peeling off my drenched jacket. "At the risk of pulling out an old cliché, let's get you out of those wet clothes."

Her lips pulled together in a frown. "We are working tonight," she reminded me, all stern and prim.

"Yes, *Mom,*" I retorted with a grin. "That doesn't mean I want you ruining my furniture with that wet dress you're wearing." A dress I would have liked to tear off. She looked good enough dry, but now she was something out of a fantasy, the fabric clinging to every curve.

Only when she shivered did I shake off my wandering train of thought and announce, "I'm sure I can find something for you upstairs."

I led the way since I wasn't sure I could keep my hands off her ass if I was behind her. I was an ass guy, and hers was second to none.

"How often do you stay here?" she asked as we climbed the winding staircase.

"Maybe a couple of nights a month." Nights like the one currently shaping up. The wind howled, and the windows rattled hard enough to make me wonder whether we'd lose power. What a great excuse to light a few candles.

What the fuck, Evan?

"I guess you have somebody to take care of it for you?" When I shot her a curious look at the top of the stairs, she shrugged. "No dust. It doesn't smell all closed up and musty."

She didn't miss anything. "I have a housekeeper who comes out once a week to keep the place aired." I led her down the hall to the suite sitting at the far end and opened the doors to my bedroom. "The closet is this way," I explained, leading her past the bed and trying like hell to fight the urge to throw her on it.

We had an entire house to ourselves and a storm raging outside. It was a recipe for all kinds of fun.

"I am so damn jealous." She let out a disbelieving laugh on entering my closet, which was roughly the size of my office at the country club. "I would kill for this kind of closet space."

I pulled out a pair of sweatpants and a faded T-shirt from the drawers where I kept casual overnight clothes. "Here. These will do. You can dry off in the bathroom if you want." I opened the adjoining door and turned on a light inside before beginning to unbutton my shirt.

She cleared her throat and looked away, but not soon enough to hide the flash of hunger in her eyes. "Thanks. I won't be long."

"You sure you don't need any help?" I offered. "I could towel you off."

She could roll her eyes all she wanted. I wasn't fooled. "I think I can manage on my own. And I wouldn't want to tire you out," she added with a teasing little grin as she swung the bathroom door shut. "Remember, you said you would help me with the seating chart."

"Of course, that was just a way to get you here."

"No shit, Sherlock. But I'm holding you to it." I couldn't be mad as I changed into sweats, looking forward to the night ahead.

～

MY ANTICIPATION COOLED when Valentina took over the dining room after printing her spreadsheets in my home office. With rain lashing the windows and lightning flickering in the distance, she looked over her work with narrowed eyes. Somehow, my clothes made her hotter than ever. She had knotted the oversized T-shirt at her waist and rolled the waistband of the sweatpants a few times so they wouldn't drag on the floor.

Just looking at her, my mind conjured up all the different ways I wanted her.

Dripping wet from the torrential downpour and spread out over my desk, my head between her thighs... licking her sweet cunt, then filling her to the hilt, hitting that spot I know she's wild for again and again until I pulled every last moan from her lips. Her fingers twisted in my hair as she screamed my name... until she was too weak to stand. Too many filthy thoughts blended one after another.

She wound her damp hair into a bun, then held it in place with a clip she had attached to the hem of the T-shirt. "Okay. Here's what we're going to do." Her voice pulled me back to reality as she picked up her tablet, balancing it on her arm. "I have a diagram of the ballroom here. I need you to read off the RSVPs we've received so far, listed on those printed spreadsheets. You'll see a number in the first column after each guest's name. Read that number off to me, too, so I can keep track."

What the fuck had I gotten myself into? "What do the numbers mean?"

"Basically, we broke the guest list down by people who can and should absolutely not under any circumstances be seated together."

"You're not serious."

She looked up at me from her screen, smirking. "Do I sound like I'm joking? There are a lot of people on the guest list and generations worth of bad blood between a few of the families and ex-friends. Everybody's known everybody forever, and some people don't know how to let go of a grudge."

"It does suck when people can't let go of things that happened a long time ago." I knew it was a mistake before it was fully out of my mouth. The stiffening of her spine only confirmed it.

"Sometimes, certain things can't be forgotten," she murmured, her voice flat. "Though, who knows? If both parties try to make amends, anything could happen."

"Listen. I'm—"

She cut me off. "Let's read off the first name." When I didn't hop to it immediately, she scowled. "What? You see how much we have to get through."

Maybe it wasn't the time. When would it be? That was the question, leaving my skin hot and itchy as we faced off from opposite sides of the table.

She had closed the door again, shutting me out. I could demand, I could shout and bully, but I knew it would get me nowhere with the most stubborn woman alive. There was nothing for me to do but look at the first of many sheets she had printed. "Anderson. Oh, that's me."

Her lips twitched. "I'm guessing we can put you down as a yes?"

"I don't think I have anything else going on that day."

She snorted, then dragged her stylus over the screen. "Next?"

"Do you want something to drink?" I asked instead of reading the next line.

"Evan," she groaned before her head fell back. "We have so many names to get through. And I need to get the place cards printed out in time for the wedding. Please, work with me here."

"I'm not trying to get you drunk and have my way with you if that's what you're worried about." We both knew I didn't need to get her drunk to make that happen anyway. "But there's nothing wrong with a little iced tea or whatever you happen to want."

Her sigh told me she'd relented. "I could use an iced tea if you have any."

I knew I would find some in the pantry, stocked up along with a handful of other essentials I liked to keep on hand. Pouring a bottle into a pair of glasses and adding ice, I carried them back to the dining room and handed one to her. "Let's keep going," she insisted instead of thanking me.

Did she think I'd let her run away the minute we were through with the seating chart? Did she know me at all? Or was she telling herself what she needed to believe?

A few minutes in, I appreciated her system. After an hour, I appreciated it even more. She had already sectioned the ballroom off into eight distinct areas, so once I read a name and a number, she dragged and dropped names into slots around the tables.

"Where did you come up with this method?" I asked about halfway through the list. There was something strangely satisfying about working together and making progress—like a team.

"The result of years of work," she explained. "Trial and error. You must know how that goes."

"It sounds vaguely familiar."

She set the tablet down for the first time since we started, shaking out her hands. "I doubt you were born knowing how to run a country club, much less how to make them as successful as you have."

"True," I agreed, admiring the way her tits swayed gently under my shirt when she leaned over the table to jot a few notes on a spreadsheet. She must have been soaked down to her bra. I wasn't about to complain. "It takes time, but once you get your system in place, it's rinse and repeat."

"How many times do you plan on rinsing and repeating?" she asked, glancing up from the pages and wearing a knowing grin.

"I've set a goal of ten properties total within the next two years." Funny. I hadn't come out and announced that to anyone. It had always been one of those secret, quiet goals. When she asked, it made perfect sense to tell her.

Her head bobbed slowly. "That's ambitious," she concluded, sounding surprised.

"You don't think I can pull it off?"

"Did I say that? Thanks for putting words in my mouth," she snapped. Was it twisted, the way I craved those flashes of temper?

"No, you didn't say that," I replied when it seemed like she was waiting for one.

"I only said it was ambitious, which it is," she concluded, capping a highlighter. "I remember a time when all you wanted was to take a no-stress job at one of your family's properties and do as little work as possible."

She never mentioned the past. I told myself not to read too much into it and simply shrugged. "I grew up."

"You clearly did. I mean, you're still a whiny little bitch who lets his cock lead him around, but you did grow up when it comes to business."

"Thanks?" I ventured, snorting.

"I might even learn to respect you one day," she decided.

"Oh, thank you. Hang on. Where the hell is my diary so I can record this moment for posterity?" Scratching my head, I looked around at the table, shifting pages around at random while she heaved a sigh.

"Have you checked up your ass?" she asked with a sweet smile. "When you find it, don't forget to add the part where I dump a glass of iced tea over your head."

"I'll be sure to add that part," I promised. Let her pretend all she wanted that she wasn't fighting a smile, but I could see through her.

"Ugh." Rolling her eyes, she muttered, "I should know better than to try to give you a compliment."

"Flatter me all you want. I'd never turn down praise, especially from you, Valentina." Her cheeks went pink, and that was all it took. I had to keep pushing. The door was open again, if only a crack. "If it makes you feel better, I'll give you a compliment. One for one."

Her head tipped to the side while she tapped a finger on the remaining spreadsheets in front of her. "We need to get back to work."

No one would believe it if I told them what happened a heartbeat later. I could have sworn on a stack of Bibles, but no way anyone who wasn't in my house at that exact moment would believe the lights flickered and then went out.

"You have got to be kidding me!" Valentina threw her arms into the air, barely visible now that the only light in the room came from her tablet and the faint, gray light outside. "Come *on!*" It was the way her voice broke that stole my breath and rattled my ribcage.

"Hey. It's okay. I'll find some candles, and we'll keep going." All she did was cover her face with her hands and turn away from me. Her shoulders were shaking, and soon, a choked sob filled the room.

A knot in my chest tightened. Forget getting candles. I went to her instead and took her by the shoulders, turning her in place. She hung her head, unwilling to look at me. "Everything will be fine. I've got you," I said reassuringly. The only thing that felt right was gathering her in my arms and holding her close to my chest, rubbing her back while murmuring, "Don't cry."

"I'm just so frustrated," she mumbled. "One more goddamn thing standing in my way."

"There isn't an obstacle in existence you couldn't charge through. You have me helping you too." I couldn't help it. She smelled so good, and her hair was so soft. I touched my nose to the top of her head and breathed in, closing my eyes. There was something comforting about having her this close, though I was supposed to be the one comforting her.

"I'm just so..." She lifted her head, her tear-filled eyes finding mine. Lightning flashed, bathing the room in its harsh glare before going dark again.

"Everything's going to be fine." I cupped her cheek with one hand, overwhelmed by the rush of hunger that had me in its grips. Every time, I could start off wanting to comfort her, only to wind up dying to fuck her. There was something I couldn't define when it came to the two of us. Something time couldn't erase.

Her tear-filled eyes searched mine. "I keep telling myself we shouldn't do this anymore," she breathed out, leaning against me. "Then you swoop in to pick me up, and I'm in your arms, and I can't remember why I ever resisted."

"Maybe you need to stop fighting yourself," I suggested. "Go with it."

I expected her to argue. To tell me how predictable I was and remind me we were supposed to be working tonight.

Since when did she do the predictable thing?

Her arms encircled my neck before I buried my face in hers, inhaling her sweetness, soaking in her warmth while I backed her against the table. With a sweep of my arm, I sent the papers flying in all directions and placed her on the table, laying her back. Running my hands down the length of her body, I took her legs and propped them against my chest before caressing her from ankle to hip, my blood humming at the feel of her supple flesh under the baggy pants.

"Tell me you know we shouldn't do this," she begged, even as she moved to tug at my pants' waistband. I was getting tired of the charade. Of her telling herself what she thought she should believe when I knew damned well she did what she wanted, and to hell with naysayers.

"Stop kidding yourself," I whispered, my dick begging to be let out of its cage and shoved deep inside her.

When she sat up, I was sure she was going to shut the whole thing down before we started. I braced myself for the disappointment, but it was short-lived. She dipped her hand under my waistband and slid down off the table to work the pants down around my thighs. My boxer briefs came next, and a flash of lightning revealed her, giving me a couple of quick strokes before bending and guiding me into her open mouth.

My eyes closed before a satisfied groan worked its way out of me.

Jesus Christ.

There was nothing like the feeling of her pouty lips wrapped around me, her tongue working my head as she moved up and down my shaft. She sucked like she was hungry for me, and maybe she was, her nails digging into my ass to hold me in place while her head rhythmically bobbed up and down. Her soft groans were a symphony, mixing with the raging wind and the thunder that rumbled hard enough to make the floor shake.

I gave myself over to it, to her, running my hands through her soft hair, letting the sensations overtake me. For somebody who swore we shouldn't do this, she sure sucked my cock as if her life depended on it. Mine sure as hell did. She held my world in her mouth, controlling me with every stroke. I was helpless against her, but then, I always had been. There was no saving myself from this.

Hell, I didn't want to be saved.

Still, when the familiar tingle began at the base of my spine, I pulled her away before I could fill her throat. If there was one thing I believed in, it was returning a favor. And tasting her delicious cunt was more of a favor to me than it was to her.

I propped her back up to the table and then lowered her sweatpants as I dropped to my knees, parting her thighs before settling between them. The aroma of her arousal left me panting, desperate for a taste.

"There is nothing in the world as perfect as this pussy," I whispered, lapping at the lace covering her dripping cunt. She had soaked through, and I caught the taste on my tongue, the flavor exploding, consuming my senses.

"Oh God, yes... don't stop... Evan!" She took my head in her hands and pressed my face into the wet lace, grinding and seeking the friction she needed, too impatient for me to pull the thong away from her glistening lips. When she rocked her hips, I nudged the thin fabric to the side, sliding my tongue into her wet, swollen folds. "Just like that. Please don't stop," she begged, losing control, hips jerking frantically before I added a finger to her beckoning entrance and drove it deep. Her hips shot up from the table, a howl piercing the air.

Her moans drove me wild.

I needed more.

I needed all of her.

I slid another finger in, driving deeper, twisting and scissoring. Finding her G-spot, I stroked it and her clit at the same time, using her reactions to guide each caress.

"Oh... God... Evan," she whispered frantically, riding my face. Using me.

Let her use me. Let her coat my tongue with her juices. I could have suffocated happily so long as the last thing I heard was her ecstatic moans and my name across her lips.

When she came, her shouts almost deafened me, the sound filling my ears while I lapped up every drop of her fragrant honey. She was exquisite.

The thought of living without her all these years had cement blocking my throat and tasting awfully close to regret.

Licking her clean, I stood, staring down at her limp, breathless body.

I did that.

And I would do it again. I had to. It was as simple as breathing and twice as necessary. I was made for this. Made for her.

Her eyes opened a clear blue that flashed brighter than any lightning. "I'm on the pill," she whispered, peeling her thong away from her body and spreading her legs again. "Fuck me. *Now.*"

This was new. Desire flooded my veins and ignited a fire within me, a fire fueled by her admission.

The head of my cock was dripping as I lined up with her drenched entrance, sinking deep. The sudden rush of sensation left me grinding my teeth, holding on for dear life. I felt every inch with no barrier between us, every ripple of her tight walls gripping me deep, promising release.

When her legs locked behind me, I rocked into her, bottoming out. She whimpered, but the look of ecstasy I saw when the lightning flashed again told me she needed this as much as I did. I pulled back, savoring the feel of her along my length, then pushed into her, taking her hard, giving her what she wanted.

The table shifted each time I slammed into her, and as pleasure claimed her again, her head rolled helplessly from side to side. "Yeeesss... more," she begged, demanded, pulling me in with her firm legs, greedy for me.

"Like this?" I asked through gritted teeth, staring down at her and watching her writhe and moan while I fought off the urge to come. Not yet, not until she screamed for me. I drove into her again, sinking as deep as I could get but still grinding into her when I couldn't go any further. "Do you like my cock buried inside you?"

"Fuck yes!" She tried sitting up, her mouth seeking mine. Suddenly, it was all I needed, and I roughly grabbed her by the nape of the neck, pulling her face up to meet mine. I gave in, stroking her tongue with mine in time with my thrusts.

Knowing she could taste herself on me heightened everything, made it more intense, and left me barely clinging to what little control I had left. I groaned in her mouth, the sensations climbing my spine and coating me slick with sweat.

The first pulse of those smooth muscles along my length threatening to squeeze me was all it took for the last thread to snap, letting go inside her, filling her until our combined juices leaked between us, leaving us both a breathless, sweating mess.

She leaned back and flashed a wicked smile before releasing a deep sigh. Did she have any idea how magnificent she was?

The storm still raged, the sound clearer once my heartbeat was no longer thudding in my ears. "Should we get back to work?" My voice was a raspy whisper.

Her soft, knowing chuckle answered my question before she spoke. "It depends on what you mean by work. I can think of a few more things I want you to do for me once I've taken a shower." Her nails trailed down my chest, sending sparks racing through me. "We might want to take it somewhere more comfortable, though."

"I've got just the place," I murmured, picking her up and carrying her out of the room to the stairs. It looked like my bed was going to get some use tonight, after all.

11

VALENTINA

There was one aspect of the wedding planning I hadn't stuck my nose in.

It was a relief to be arriving as a guest and not the planner at Rose's shower. It was taking place in the Goldsmiths' SoHo penthouse late on a Sunday morning, two weeks before the wedding. Sienna had planned everything relating to the shower, and now I rode the elevator up to the top floor, carrying a basket full of wrapped gifts after having gone through Rose's wedding registry and snagging all of the smaller pieces. I regretted my tactic as soon as it came time to wrap ten individual boxes, but the effect was nice, right down to the cascading ribbon and fresh flowers I'd tucked in here and there.

If anything, it would be nice to spend an afternoon among women without the threat of male distraction getting in my way. I had a hard enough time keeping Evan and me a secret, not that there was an Evan and me, technically. There was only what we were doing together. I had to stay clear on that, or else risk complications I didn't have the time or energy to deal with.

Somehow, he still managed to worm his way into my thoughts as I stepped off the elevator. He was supposed to be golfing with the guys today, sort of a preview of what they could expect in two short weeks.

Two weeks.

The idea made my stomach queasy, but things were going according to schedule. We even got the bulk of the seating chart finished at Evan's, albeit on Saturday morning after the storm had passed. The rest of the time had been spent doing just about anything but working. Since then, we'd both been too busy to see each other, meaning I'd been replaying that night in my head like a favorite movie. All things considered, it was a much safer course of action than actually sleeping with him again.

My skin went warm when I remembered how wild it was, going crazy on each other while thunder rumbled and lightning flashed. When my clit started to pulse, I had to deliberately push the memories out of my mind before ringing the bell. No room for erotic fantasies at a bridal shower, especially when my family would be there.

"Come in!" Olivia was radiant, beaming, kissing my cheek before draping an arm around my waist and leading me deeper into the penthouse she shared with her husband. "There are already a few dozen girls here. We'll wait another few minutes to see who else straggles in."

The spacious living room was full of chatty, giggling women. Fresh flowers in Rose's wedding colors of cream, navy, and peach were scattered around, along with balloons and streamers decorating the overloaded gift table spanning the far side of the room.

"What can I do to help?" I asked, raising my voice to be heard over dozens of overlapping voices. I wished I had thought to bring ibuprofen for the headache already threatening to break loose in the back of my head. I was used to spending time in large crowds, noisy and boisterous, and usually half-drunk. There was something different about the decibel level and frequency reached by a group of excited women that somehow topped that.

Olivia shook her head as I placed the basket among countless other beautifully wrapped gifts. "Absolutely not, young lady. You are here to enjoy yourself today. You have already done so much and deserve a little break."

"At least tell me where I can find the guest of honor." The shower wasn't a surprise—some things had to be left by the wayside with a schedule this tight. There was no time to sneak around and pretend we weren't having a party.

"She's in her old room, resting a little." I must have looked as worried as I felt since Olivia shook her head and waved a hand. "She's fine. Still a little green around the gills, but nothing serious. Aria is in there with her now."

It would be a break from all the voices and laughter that were like an ice pick in my ears, and I couldn't understand why as I walked down the hall leading to a room I had stayed in more times over the years than I could count. Our parents were always getting us together back in the day, having little parties and dinners. When things ran late, we would spend the night.

Rose was lying down when I eased the door open, and Aria turned my way from her seat on the edge of the bed. "There you are. I was wondering when you were going to get here."

"What a welcome," I grumbled, ignoring her and going straight to Rose. "How's it going?"

"I'll be fine once I get a little rest." She closed her eyes, and I exchanged a worried look with my sister.

"You should see who's out there waiting for you." I sat

across from Aria on Rose's left side. "I don't know if you're going to have room in your apartment for everything on that gift table."

"We don't need anything," Rose pointed out with a faint smile. "I only did the registry because Mom said it was tradition."

"Everybody likes to shower the bride with gifts before a wedding," Aria insisted. "I'm a little jealous, honestly."

"Tell me about it," I joked. "I saw somebody bought the espresso machine. I'd be happy to break it in for you."

We had Rose giggling before long. By the time Olivia tapped on the door to check in, she was sitting up and looking stronger.

It was wrong of me to think about myself at a time like this, walking behind my sister as we followed Rose from the room so she could greet her guests. None of this had to do with me, yet there was no hope of avoiding the memories that wouldn't leave me the hell alone.

For the second day in a row, I wasn't sick. The morning sickness that had first tipped me off to my pregnancy had miraculously gone away, and I was feeling better than I had in weeks as I got up on what seemed like an average Friday morning. Aria and I were going home for the weekend after our last classes of the day at Columbia since Mom was having a hard time adjusting to us being gone in the weeks since school started.

"You can do your laundry here," she'd offered to sweeten the deal. Any college student knew how important that was.

It wasn't until I stopped at the ladies' room between classes that I noticed there was anything wrong.

Standing back, I watched Rose's guests surround her, squealing and giggling, all of them telling her how beautiful she looked and asking about the baby. The strange, almost sick sensation that had washed over me at the engagement party worked its magic again. Somebody sucked the air out of the room while a cold, sick sweat coated the back of my neck. "I'm going to see if Sienna needs help," I told Aria, escaping to the kitchen like my life depended on it.

No, no. Not like this, please. I didn't know what to do. I hadn't even been to the doctor yet. I hadn't figured out how to tell my parents, and now I was bleeding.

"Hey, you." Sienna and a couple of Rose's friends finished setting up a tray of drinks, which one of the girls carried into the living room. "You look a little flustered," she informed me after looking me up and down.

"I'm okay. It's just... a lot out there." I winced, and she giggled.

"I know. My ears are ringing, and I'm not in the room with them. So long as Rose is happy," she concluded, refilling a tray of pastry wrapped something or other from a tray she took out of the oven. "I covered the catering, but why I didn't think to hire servers for this, I have no idea."

"Because you've got me here, obviously." It was something to do, and I needed something else to focus on. "Put me to work."

"Do you ever just relax and enjoy yourself?" she asked, handing me the platter of hors d'oeuvres. "Knock yourself out if it means that much to you."

"What a strange way to say thank you," I muttered, making her laugh as I left the room. Was I turning into Evan, deflecting with humor whenever things got too uncomfortable?

"I can't wait until you pop," one of the girls gushed to Rose as I wound my way through the room. "You are going to be the cutest little pregnant lady ever."

"Where's that hunky fiancé?" another girl asked. There were so many unfamiliar faces that I was a little lost. Rose had a lot of friends from work, both girls who modeled for the company and girls who worked in the offices. It was a real family environment.

"The men were forbidden from showing their faces," Aunt Lourde announced. "Now, why don't we start opening gifts?" The applause the idea earned told me everybody was eager to get started.

"We should've made this a double shower," somebody suggested while I gathered napkins and empty plates to take back to the kitchen. "For the wedding and the baby. Two birds with one stone."

Something was wrong. I had told myself for hours that everything would be fine, but everything was anything but by Friday night. I only wanted it to be. Once I got so dizzy, I hit the bathroom floor. Aria heard me and opened the door even when I told her not to. There was no way to hide it now.

After hours of pain, I didn't want to.

"Swear to me." I squeezed her hand until she winced. "Swear you will never, ever tell anybody about this."

"What if you need to go to a hospital?" She looked so scared, eyes wide, and face pale. She looked a lot like me, come to think of it, remembering my ashen complexion when I caught my reflection in the bathroom mirror after she helped me to my feet and practically carried me to bed.

"If it doesn't slow down by morning, I'll go to the hospital," I promised. "But I don't want to go unless I really, really have to. Okay? Please," I whispered, squeezing her hand even harder.

"Why didn't you tell me?" she asked quietly, with tears choking her.

"I don't know. I didn't know how to tell you. And now..." All I could do was lie down and curl into a ball as the finality of what was happening washed over me. There was no baby anymore.

The baby I didn't know what to do about, the baby I was unsure of, was gone.

Now I knew how much I had wanted it.

Her.

There was no way of knowing if I was having a girl or a boy, but somehow, I was sure I'd just lost my daughter.

"I'm going to stay with you." She crawled into bed beside me, pulling the blankets up over both of us before wrapping an arm around me. "You don't have to tell me anything you don't want to. Just one thing, though. Does the father know?"

I couldn't hold back the sob that tore through me when I thought of Evan. We hadn't spoken in three weeks, ever since he left for Harvard. He'd tried to reach out through texts and calls, but I didn't bother answering. Not that he ever said anything substantial or meaningful.

***Evan:** Talk to me, we can work this out, I'm behind whatever you decide to do.*

Something between us had shattered the night I told him about the baby. He was like a different person, a friendly acquaintance instead of the guy I spent the summer sleeping with after knowing him for four years.

"He knows," I eventually whispered when the crushing pain passed.

She must've known better than to ask who he was because she didn't bother. I doubted she had any guesses. We had kept things quiet. There I was, thinking he wanted to keep our group from blowing up if they knew we were sleeping together, but I knew differently. He never intended for us to be more than a fling —somebody to fuck around with before he moved on with his actual life in college.

And after I told him the following morning, I knew for sure he was more relieved than anything else. He didn't feel sorry for me.

He didn't feel sorry for what we had lost. The complication was out of the way.

I couldn't be here anymore. All those laughing, happy women in the other room. All they did was remind me of what was irreparably broken inside me. I would never be like them because I would never be able to let go of the pain. I hadn't processed it. I had only covered it up, shoved it down deep, and now it was exposed like a raw nerve after having a tooth pulled. Every little thing that brushed it made it throb with unimaginable pain.

"Sweetie?" My head snapped up at the sound of my mother's voice, and I had never been so glad to see her. Why hadn't I told her about this before? She would understand now. I knew she would. Mom always understood.

She crossed the room, arms extended. "You're ready to drop. I knew you were working too hard on the wedding," she fretted, even touching the back of her hand to my forehead like she was checking for a fever. "You should go to Rose's room and lie down. I would hate to see you miss all the fun out there, but you need to take care of yourself. Rose will understand."

I longed to tell her. The words were right there, on the tip of my tongue. But it would only ruin things for Mom in the end. She was so happy for Rose and Colton and thrilled for Olivia and Lourde. This was no time to overshadow that.

"I think I am a little burned out," I agreed, nodding slowly, taking sips of air through the pinhole my throat had tightened into. "I might go home, honestly. I didn't think it would hit me like this."

"Honey, by all means. And hey," she whispered, taking my face in her hands. "Your sister would love to pitch in wherever she can. So would I, for that matter. These final weeks are going to be so hectic. Please, let us help you if we can, all right? The wedding won't be any good if you can't enjoy it."

At this rate, I wondered if I would ever be able to enjoy anything. There was something broken in me, so broken I didn't know if it was possible to fix it. Any ability to compartmentalize was gone. I had lost control of myself and was spiraling in a way I never had.

"I'll take it easy when I can," I promised, though, of course, I didn't mean a word of it. Sometimes, a girl had to tell her mother what she needed to hear.

Nobody else noticed me slipping out while Rose tore into another one of her many gifts. Life was so fucking unfair. One of my best, lifelong friends, somebody who had never been anything but supportive and sweet, and I didn't have it in me to stick around for her shower because I was too busy feeling sorry for myself.

If only it were really that simple. The fact was, I couldn't handle the reminder of what had almost been mine.

And how I didn't know how much I wanted it until it was all gone.

12

EVAN

"What do you think?" I asked Colton as we strode toward the clubhouse after finishing our game. "Do we have what it takes to impress everybody the weekend of the wedding?"

We'd just finished eighteen holes on a glorious Sunday, and I was flying high. The wedding was two weeks out, plans were being finalized, and already word had spread of the influential Black and Goldsmith families choosing my country club for the site of a gala wedding. Serena was up to her neck in inquiries with curious callers asking to reserve space all the way into next year.

The only thing dampening my spirits was my best friend's scowl when I turned his way. "We have a problem," he announced, lifting his sunglasses to give me a narrow-eyed stare.

My stomach dropped. "What is it?"

"Why the fuck did you never invite us out here to play before now?" He barely managed to get it out before laughing.

Noah, Miles, and Lucian cracked up at what must have

been relief written all over my face. "You never asked for an invitation," I reminded him, giving his shoulder a firm but friendly punch as we continued across the emerald lawn separating my two businesses.

It was a gorgeous day, perfect spring weather, and the pleasant buzzing of bees and fluttering of birds added to the sweet smell of fresh-cut grass and what was already coming to life in the gardens we cut through on our way up to the clubhouse dining room. It was downright idyllic, and I'd made it happen. Not the weather, but everything else.

"I remember visiting out here when we were kids. Senior year," Noah recalled. "Your dad treated us to a game next door to the club, remember?"

"That was before your family owned the golf course?" Miles asked.

"My family never owned the golf course. I owned it," I explained. "My father never had the vision." He never had a lot of things.

We reached the rear veranda and Colton turned around, folding his arms as he scanned what stretched out in front of us. "It's perfect," he declared. "Look at that lake. I'd love to take a boat out on it."

He then pointed to an unused lot on the other side of the lake, overgrown but still picturesque. "You ever think about buying that lot? You could put up a hotel. Create an entire resort experience for your guests."

"Let me guess," Lucian joked. "The Black family would oversee construction."

"What's wrong with that?" he asked while the rest of us laughed.

"I thought about it," I confessed, waving everyone inside. It was a beautiful day, but what I needed more than anything was a cold drink after spending hours in the sun.

"He'll have more than enough on his plate once photos from the wedding get published," Lucian guessed as we took seats at the bar opposite the windows overlooking the gardens. There were a couple of men in polo shirts like ours parked on stools who raised a hand in greeting, and most of the tables throughout the dining room were in use. It was a bustling afternoon, and every sale rung up at the register was sweet music to my ears.

"Mr. Anderson." Right away, I recognized Serena's breathless voice, along with the level of stress it held when she found me.

"Who is this?" Lucian turned on his stool, putting on a charming smile while he sized her up. I wanted to tell him to take his attention elsewhere. She was my most trusted employee, and I couldn't afford her complaining about being harassed by one of my best friends.

Thankfully, she was too interested in whatever made her approach us to pay much attention to him. "This is Serena, my event coordinator," I explained. Turning away from him, I asked her, "What can I help you with? I thought you were only stopping in for a few minutes this morning."

"I was until I ran into someone." She gulped, lowering her voice to a whisper. "He's been waiting up in your office for an hour and a half. I would've called to tell you, but he insisted on keeping it a surprise."

"There he is." My father's voice rang out, stabbing me in the ears and making me cringe before I composed myself. Son of a bitch. He strutted across the dining room, his white hair gleaming in the sunlight, turning him into a beacon as he passed between tables.

Fuck me. The man had a sixth sense when it came to destroying a good time. My skin crawled, and my stomach churned, but I couldn't let it show.

"Dad. I thought you were in Morocco until next month." Incredible, the way the sight of him could take what had been a great day and turn it into something cringe-inducing.

"Your mother's still there, shopping her way through the country." He offered a brief handshake before turning to the guys. I was only half aware of Miles introducing himself, of Colton asking how business had been lately. Why, of all times, did he have to show up now?

I knew why, and the answer didn't provide any comfort. What he wanted more than anything was to find out I'd run the place into the ground. He had never expected me to make a success out of this, much less on the scale I'd managed it. Anyone could sit back and do the bare minimum, letting a business run itself with the help of countless assistants and underlings. I was the one who had the balls and the vision to do more than coast by the way he always had.

And he couldn't fucking stand it.

He could smile all he wanted, but there was no hiding that hard glint in his eye. Sizing things up, judging, looking for any excuse to put me down. To make sure my head didn't get too big. One of his favorite sayings, one of many empty statements I'd heard so many times, they became a mantra I repeated to myself whenever I lost sight of how deeply I needed to succeed.

"Obviously, nothing as busy as this." He clapped a hand on my shoulder in response to Colton's question, and it took everything I had not to shake him off. "But we aren't all business geniuses like this one."

"Careful with that genius talk," Lucian warranted him with a grin. "We don't want him getting an even bigger opinion of himself."

"I'm not sure that would be possible." Dad shone his

friendly, affable smile on me, and I hoped for my friends' sake that my grimace looked like a smile.

"Let him have a huge opinion of himself," Colton insisted, grinning my way. "So long as it means my wedding goes off without a hitch. Mr. Anderson, we expected you would still be out of the country, or else we would have—"

"No need to explain," Dad told him with a hearty laugh. "Congratulations, by the way. If I hadn't gotten so damn bored of all that shopping at this bazaar and that market, I would still be over there. I suspect I'll have to fly back soon, anyway, to make sure my wife doesn't bankrupt me."

Relief cooled the heat spreading through my chest. Good. He wouldn't be here to ruin things. Here I was, close to thirty years old, and the man still had the power to get under my skin. He was the sort of man who used to brag about scheming his way out of doing chores when he was a kid, who couldn't understand when I first approached him with suggestions on how to improve his business. All because some of us studied and learned in college rather than going through the motions.

I knew something else about him that my friends didn't. He held a lifelong contempt toward people like them, though he would never show it outside his immediate family. He had grown up with the stigma of being new money, and as an adult, he'd been rich enough to own and run country clubs but not wealthy enough to count the members among his friends. We had nothing like the fortune the Diamond and Black families had amassed. Enough to afford a long trip to Morocco but not enough to send me to an exclusive prep school like the one I'd attended. Only a scholarship had made that possible. Maybe he would have made enough money and then some if he had only tried to do more than skate by.

As always, his hypocrisy made my skin crawl. "Why don't we go to my office... have a chat?" I suggested, getting up from my seat.

"No, that's fine," he insisted. "I don't want to take you away from your guests. I've been waiting so long, I'm almost late for an appointment as it is. We'll have to catch up soon." With another handshake, he was gone, his white hair disappearing around the corner as he approached the lobby. It was just like him, popping in to remind me he existed, then leaving without explaining what the hell was so important in the first place.

I picked up my iced tea, the taste of which brought Valentina to mind—the iced tea we drank at my house before the power went out then what played out after. "What time was the shower scheduled for?" I asked no one in particular, playing it off like a casual question.

The guys exchanged glances, knowing exactly why I abruptly changed the topic. Except for Miles, who was new to the group, they knew enough about our uncomfortable history to leave it alone. His mouth snapped shut when Lucian shot him a look.

"I think it started around eleven," Colton replied.

"It will probably go on for hours," Noah predicted with a smirk. "Get a bunch of women together, talking about weddings and babies, and you're talking about an all-day event."

"Thinking about going over there and looking for some fresh blood?" Lucian inquired with a knowing grin. "I was thinking along those lines, myself."

"Do you ever stop thinking about pussy?" Miles asked.

"No," Lucian deadpanned, earning a laugh from the rest of the group. I did my best, but it came off as half-hearted and empty. I needed to see Valentina.

All it took was a few minutes with my father to stir up a lifetime of bullshit. She was the only one who knew what things were really like with him. The way he looked down on my friends while kissing their asses, along with their fathers' asses, of course. The hypocrisy was endless. How could a man who'd had everything handed to him resent Colton and the others for living the same way? And unlike my friends, Dad had never bothered going above and beyond. He had built nothing of his own. I had no doubt it ate at him as much as anything else.

Valentina would understand. She always had.

I stared down at my phone, waffling between texting her and letting it go. What could she do, after all? *She could listen.* So could my living room wall. A wall could do roughly as much for me as she could anyway. Nothing would change once I'd vented like a whiny child.

Still, the impulse was surprisingly intense. What would it be like to have someone to go home to after being bombarded?

"Oh. That's a shame." It was Miles who spoke first, nodding down at his screen. "Aria says Valentina wasn't feeling well and left before Rose finished opening gifts."

"I hope she isn't overdoing it," Colton murmured with a frown. "I was worried this would be too much for her. Why does she always work like she has something to prove?"

"Because she always feels like she has something to prove," I observed without hesitation. One of the many points on which we had always been able to relate. I knew now that deep in the back of my mind, I had always observed her success through the lens of the time we spent getting to know each other that one wild summer.

There's Valentina, proving herself. That was what drove her.

I kept my thoughts to myself until we went out to our cars, with the guys climbing into the limo I'd sent out to the city to pick them up while I got behind the wheel of my Mercedes. Before setting out, I sent Valentina a text.

Me: *Heard you weren't feeling well earlier. Can I bring you something? I could stop by and drop off whatever you need.*

There wasn't a woman in existence who'd ever deserved this level of attention. Not from me. Here I was, wanting to drive back to the city and act as a gofer to someone more than capable of taking care of herself.

I couldn't help but blame it on my father, whose contact I pulled up after getting on I-95 and finding myself stuck in road work traffic. He answered right away, his voice filling the car and mysteriously devoid of the boisterous energy it held earlier. "Now you have time for me." His sigh didn't hide the animosity he held.

He always had a way of twisting shit around. "I had no idea you were there. I would've come straight up to see you otherwise."

"I'm sure you would have rather spent the afternoon with your friends. Not that it matters," he continued with another sigh. "I couldn't announce in front of them what I came all this way to tell you. Your mother plans on staying with friends in Italy once she's tired of Morocco. She's not coming home."

What a good thing I was stuck in place, surrounded by cars going nowhere, since the sudden shock might have been a problem if I'd been driving at speed. "What? Since when?"

"We've agreed to a divorce," he explained, flat and even. No emotion spared for a woman he'd been married to for thirty years. "I came home to take care of things with the lawyers. This isn't something you want to handle long-distance. I'm sure she'll call you at some point."

I wasn't so sure. She never wanted to be a mother. *A kid knows when they're an unwelcome guest in their own home.* "It's a shame this is happening," I offered, staring straight ahead while countless memories of stiff, distant holidays and strained smiles for family photos raced through my head. All it did was remind me of what a disaster I'd be as a husband and parent without a strong example of either.

"These things happen," he reasoned. "At any rate, you have more than enough on your plate without worrying about us. I'll let you go. I'm having a drink with my lawyers shortly."

That was it. No goodbye, no wondering how I'd take the news. Not that I was important in all of this. I wasn't a child either. There were no illusions when it came to them and their chilly attitude toward each other.

Traffic had started moving by the time the phone buzzed with a text from Valentina, who I'd almost forgotten after being blindsided by my father for the second time in an hour.

Valentina: *I am really not feeling well and wouldn't be good company. I have everything I need. I'll see you Thursday for the final menu approval.*

I didn't have it in me to argue and knew it would be a waste of time. She was doing me a favor in the end. Cutting me off before I could show up at her apartment door looking for the comfort I'd been missing all my life.

All my life except for the summer we spent together.

13

VALENTINA

The wedding was a week and a half away now, and I couldn't sleep for more than an hour at a time without waking up in a panic, remembering something else that had to be done in these final days.

I had never dreaded something while still looking forward to it as much as this last meeting in Evan's office. It would be good to finalize a few things with him and make sure everything was on track. This meant we absolutely, positively could not fall into the same damn trap we always did, no matter that it had been more than two weeks since the last time we were together at his place during the storm.

One of us had to be smarter, and it had to be me. There was no way we were continuing this after the wedding. We couldn't. I couldn't. The past several weeks had screwed me up enough as it was.

Then there was Rose and the baby. We would have to clear the air eventually. I couldn't keep breaking down the way I was. I would have to eventually tell Evan how much he'd hurt me back then, though I didn't have the words to express it. He needed to hear that I didn't trust him to understand and couldn't handle the possibility of being rejected again, the way he'd brushed me aside and treated me like an inconvenience when I told him about the baby. I couldn't risk finding out he had truly never cared the way I cared about him.

I owed it to myself to set things straight. But now wasn't the time, not with the wedding so close and so much hanging in the balance.

I would be in and out. We could be professional. He had to know how hectic our schedule was now that we were so close to the end. No doubt he was busy too. We both had more than this single event to manage.

It didn't matter how many times I told myself to be good and stick to my guns. I couldn't ignore the way my heart rate spiked as I climbed out of the car after pulling into the lot at the country club. He would be waiting for me upstairs, maybe even watching me from the window. I was no better than a teenager with a crush as I entered the clubhouse, heading straight for the stairs leading to the second-floor offices. My heart beat a little faster with every step, telling me I'd have to force myself to get a grip.

His assistant's desk was empty when I approached his closed office door. Maybe he was in there with her. I tapped tentatively against the door with my nails, listening for any voices coming from inside. "Come in!" was all I heard, Evan's voice ringing out loud and clear and maybe a bit tight. Tense.

I eased the door open and found him sitting at his desk, his jacket slung over the back of his chair, his shirt sleeves rolled up. "Come in, make yourself comfortable," he grunted out, staring at his computer screen.

Dammit, how was he even hotter now? All absorbed by his work, scowling as he forcefully typed a message.

"What did that poor keyboard ever do to you?" I asked, crossing the room and taking a seat. I couldn't stop staring at him the entire way. His jaw was tight enough to crack a walnut, his nostrils flared, and his eyes narrowed at the screen.

"It's not a big deal," he explained, though the rigid set of his jaw told a different story. He was pissed, fighting to hold his temper, which shouldn't have turned me on the way it did. He was never so much fun as he was when he lost control. Right now, he was teetering on the edge, and the crackling energy pouring off him was an aphrodisiac.

What the hell was I thinking? I had to be better than this. I owed it to myself. "Is there anything I can help with?"

He shook his head, pounding a few more keys before tapping his trackpad. "I was emailing my father's lawyer in response to a message they sent this morning."

His father.

There weren't many topics that could piss him off as easily or as thoroughly as that man. I didn't really know him. It wasn't like Evan had brought me around to meet the family, even when we were sneaking off together whenever we had the chance that one summer. Still, I had heard about him repeatedly, incessantly. And it didn't look like time had eased any of the resentment.

"What's going on?" I asked, forgetting work for a minute when he looked at me with what could only be described as rage written across his face. Something else that time hadn't erased was the impulse to comfort him when I could.

"Dad showed up here on Sunday to tell me he and Mom are divorcing."

"Oh, my God," I whispered. Divorce after thirty years

wasn't common. How did a couple decide they'd made a mistake after three decades?

He waved off my concern with a scowl. "The lawyers actually think I give a shit about what this could do to my trust. The divorce settlement, I mean. Dad might have to shift assets around, break the trust, restructure it."

"They emailed to tell you that?"

He nodded, growling. "And I told them to get fucked if they think I give a shit about the money. I have more than enough." He slammed himself back in his chair with a grunt. "I wouldn't be surprised if this was a way for him to find out how comfortable I am. Like he expects me to scream and throw a fit like some spoiled trust fund baby. He won't come right out and ask how much I'm making here, so he has to find another way."

"I know there isn't exactly a lot of love lost between you two, but do you really think he would go this far just to see how well you've done?"

"I don't fucking know." Pushing back from the desk, he threw his hands in the air. He looked and sounded hopeless, almost defeated. Only his father could do that to him.

I thought back on all the nights he had poured his heart out to me, especially when it came to getting ready to leave for Harvard. Any parent would have been elated to know their son was attending such a prestigious school that he had worked hard enough to earn a place there. All Thomas Anderson could do was make snarky comments about his son, thinking he was too good for the rest of the family now that he was going off to school. The man was a mystery, even more so than his son.

But he would never come straight out and admit how he felt or how much he resented Evan for being a success. *"It's not in our DNA,"* Evan used to tell me. *"We don't talk about things like your family does."*

"I'm sorry," I offered. What did a person say to a full-grown adult whose parents were getting a divorce?

He ran a hand through his hair, the too-long waves flopping against his forehead as he heaved a sigh. "Thanks. It's stupid of me to let him get to me like this. I know it. It's just... there's never any way to prepare for his bullshit. I always feel like I get caught with my pants down, you know?"

Weren't we supposed to be discussing the wedding? I just couldn't bring myself to ignore what he was going through. Comforting him again.

"Remember that time you came over to our apartment after you had that fight with him?" I asked, going warm at the memory. "I told you it would be okay because nobody was home?"

For the first time since I entered the office, he grinned. It took him no time to recall the night in question. "I remember your dad's study," he replied, his smile going wider while I blushed at the memory. "I couldn't believe you wanted to do it right then and there on his desk."

"If I remember correctly, he sort of pissed me off that day. I don't remember what it was about," I admitted. "But I remember thinking how funny it was."

"It wouldn't have been so funny if he'd caught us," he pointed out, wincing.

"But he didn't. If memory serves me correctly, it was pretty fucking hot." Hot enough that my heart fluttered a little when I thought back.

I cleared my throat, breaking eye contact when I looked in my bag. We were not doing this today. We couldn't keep going through the same chain of events every time we got together. My pussy would have to deal with going unattended today. "Anyway, we really do have to get to work."

"Sure," he agreed with a sarcastic snort. "Now that I have a hard-on."

"You're the one who brought up what we did that night," I pointed out. "I was only remembering having you come over to hang out so you wouldn't punch a hole in a wall or something."

"You were the one who went down on me while I was sitting in your dad's chair." He lowered his brow along with his voice. "You taught me a lesson that night. The possibility of getting caught makes things so much hotter."

Why did he have to keep going with this? And why was it so damn effective? He was a drug, demanding I turn my back on everything that mattered in favor of one more hit.

It was getting undeniably warmer in his office. "That was a long time ago," I reminded him, fighting the urge to fan myself once my body went from warm to hot.

"Not so long," he countered. I knew the look in his dark, soulful eyes. It did unspeakable things to me, made me squeeze my legs together in a pitiful attempt at satisfying my throbbing clit. *Not today. Not again. No matter how good it will be or how much you think you need it. Shut this down, leave the building.*

An idea started swirling in my overheated mind, shoving aside the voice of reason, screaming at me to walk out before I degraded myself yet again. To think, I used to criticize the hell out of him and the other guys for letting their dicks do the thinking for them.

I was no better than they were once I let my clit lead me deeper into what I knew would only end up hurting. "I'll tell you what," I suggested. "For every question you answer, I'll give you a treat as a reward."

His eyebrows shot up. "Is that so, Valentina? Well, I could definitely work with that."

"I had a feeling you could." He watched closely as I stood and crossed his office. "First, let me do what we couldn't do in Dad's study." I flipped the lock on the door, and he laughed.

"Yeah, finding a locked door would've been a dead give-away we were up to something," he recalled, slouching now with his legs spread wide.

"Now." One slow step at a time, I crossed the room, tingling at the way his gaze raked over my body. "Let's begin. Did you confirm the delivery time on the cake?"

He offered a smirk that heated my blood. "Affirmative."

"Good." In response, I lifted the hem of my knee-length dress up to my hips, turning a full circle so he could admire my ass. He always did like it.

"That's not enough," he grunted out when I lowered the dress.

"Patience," I murmured. This was already too much fun. His dick was hard, jutting straight out from his lap. I gave it a pointed look before meeting his gaze again. Desire flickered behind his eyes, momentarily distracting me from my line of questioning. "That's not going anywhere."

"You're the devil." He sighed, making me giggle.

"Next question. Are all the plans confirmed for the yacht rental on Friday afternoon?" We'd agreed on a fishing trip for the men, one of the suggestions given while brain-storming at my apartment.

"The yacht leaves at noon. Let's see those tits," he suggested, staring at my chest.

"Excuse me, but when did you get the idea you were calling the shots?" I shook my head and clicked my tongue. "No treat this time. You'll learn."

"Jesus, Valentina..." He grabbed hold of his bulge. "See what you're doing to me? Much more of this, and there'll be a wet spot on the front of my pants."

"Poor baby," I replied with a pout, rounding the desk and straddling his lap. "Everything's set for the fireworks finale at ten?"

"The sky will be bright as day." His attention lingered on my legs, his tongue darting over his lips as he watched my hand trailing down to the inside of my thighs, my thumb rubbing against my wet seam. It was too easy to turn him into a slobbering fool.

"Good to know." I stood again, quickly sliding out of my skimpy panties and dropping them into his lap. "And we're all set with the tent and second dance floor on the lawn?"

"Yes, yes, everything's settled." He was too busy picking up my panties and holding them to his nose to say much else. My blood turned to lava once he inhaled my scent and growled like an animal. There was nothing like working him into a frenzy. Eighteen, twenty-eight, it didn't matter. He was just as helpless now as he had ever been and much hotter. Dammit, I was meant to be calling the shots here, and yet I was as helpless as him.

"And your kitchen staff is aware of the few dietary restrictions?" I asked.

"Fuck, yes," he whispered, lowering the panties to his lap again, using the delicate fabric to grind against. He stared at the apex of my thighs once I propped myself on the desk and began spreading them. His jaw tightened while a soft grunt stirred in his throat. For me. I did this to him.

"Good boy." Leaning forward, I grabbed him by his tie and pulled him close, directing him to my waiting pussy while I propped my feet on the arms of his chair. God help me, I loved this too much. I always had. "Now, you get to eat dessert."

The wicked grin that flashed over his face reminded me too much of the boy he used to be before he pushed my dress up and descended on me.

14

EVAN

This was it—what we had worked for all these weeks. Considering the short timeline was such a pain in the ass, why did it feel like we'd been putting the wedding together for a year? That could've had something to do with how much had changed in the weeks between the engagement announcement and now, three days before the wedding, when the bridal party and close family and friends were due to arrive at The Delamar.

I strode into the pleasant, well-appointed hotel lobby, wheeling a suitcase behind me and carrying my wedding suit over one arm. The dry cleaner had delivered it to my office earlier, an arrangement set up by Valentina. One less errand to worry about. She'd thought of everything.

A pair of perky, blonde clerks stood up a little straighter behind the front desk when I approached. "Are you here to check in, sir?" one of the girls asked, bright and chipper. Behind her, on a credenza, sat a handful of baskets tied with peach and navy ribbon. There was only one reason they would exist.

"I'm Evan Anderson," I explained. "I have a room in the Goldsmith-Black wedding block."

"Yes, we know who you are, sir." The first girl smiled then typed on her keyboard while the other noticed me eyeing the baskets and turned to them, clasping hands over her chest. "Aren't they cute? They're full of so many neat little things. Whoever assembled them put so much work into it."

I had no doubt Valentina had stayed up late putting together personalized gift baskets for everyone in the wedding party besides herself. That was her way. "There are only a few left," I noted. "Does that mean the guests are arriving?"

"Yes, sir." The first girl tapped again on the keyboard, leaning in and squinting at her screen. "Only a few haven't checked in yet."

"And who might that be?"

"Mr. Young, Miss Miller, Mr. and Mrs. Diamond."

Miss Miller. The skin on the back of my neck tingled. "Would that be Aria Miller or Valentina Miller?"

"Valentina dropped off the gift baskets," the second clerk pointed out with a grin. "She and her assistant, that is."

Right. She had mentioned during one of our email exchanges that Bianca would be staying at the hotel over the weekend, too, to give her a chance to spend time with the wedding party instead of running around like a headless chicken. "Which room is she in?" I asked as casually as I could. "I have a few last-minute things to talk over with her. The wedding's being held at my country club."

"I probably shouldn't tell you that..." she whispered.

Why was I explaining myself to them? I had every right to ask what room a friend was staying in.

My mouth curved up into a seductive smile. "But you will."

Her eyes dart toward her co-worker then back up at me, her teeth raking across her bottom lip as her cheeks tinged pink.

Both girls giggled. "She's in room 321." I accepted my room key, tucked in a tiny envelope marked 302, and thanked them before turning toward the bank of elevators near the hotel entrance.

"Wait a second!" One of the girls held up a basket, and I chuckled before accepting it. Of course, there was one for me. A cursory glance at the contents revealed a weekend itinerary, a monogrammed flask, a pair of cufflinks, and a bottle of Johnnie Walker Blue Label. My favorite brand. *She thought of everything.*

I smiled to myself on my way across the lobby, determined to visit her room after settling in.

The past week felt like a month. It was like being a kid with a crush all over again. When I wasn't with her, she was all I could think about. When I was with her, I couldn't keep my hands off her. Every chance I had to be with her, I had to take. I wasn't sure how to process it.

Which was why I didn't bother settling into my room, merely leaving my things on the bed before heading down the hall. If I ran into anyone from the group, I could easily explain away my visit as being wedding-related. Last-minute confirmations, touching base, nothing out of the ordinary. I had waited endless days to set eyes on her again and wouldn't let our secret keep us apart.

I couldn't remember another woman who ever held my attention this long, much less to the point where I could barely function, with thoughts of her invading my awareness no matter the time of day or what was going on. She was always there. I always wanted her.

My heart pounded with every step I took down the long, quiet hallway. Days of waiting and yearning were about to pay off.

I rapped on the door at the other end of the hall, palms sweating, heart racing painfully. "Give me a second!" Valentina called out from inside. I didn't hear any other voices, giving me hope she was alone.

She wasn't sharing her room with Bianca, was she? That would put a serious crimp in my plans, not that I had any beyond taking her up against the door until she wept with pleasure.

What was I going to do when we didn't have the excuse to sneak off together? She opened the door a couple of inches, the chain in place. Nothing could have pleased me more than the smile that spread across her face when she found me waiting in the hall. "I was wondering if you would show up." She closed the door to remove the chain, then opened it again so I could enter.

"Nice room," I observed, noting the queen-sized bed. Things were looking up. "You have it all to yourself?"

"No, the entire wedding party is sharing the bed with me. You'll have to sleep at the foot. Hope you don't mind." She was rolling her eyes when she turned away from the door, the chain in place again.

"I think the guy with the lowest seniority should sleep at the foot of the bed," I countered, eyeing a stack of notecards piled on the dresser. "That would mean Miles."

"That works too. But you'll have to explain it to my sister." Her smile was brief, and now I noticed the fatigue in her eyes, in the worried little frown she wore.

"Hey." I placed my hands on her shoulders, waiting for

her to lift her head and look me in the eye. Even worked to the point of exhaustion, she was gorgeous in a soft, lilac sundress, her hair wound in a braid hanging over her shoulder. "We're almost there. Only a few more days. Then, you ought to take a little time for yourself. Decompress. You've earned it."

"Right. We both know how likely that is." She rolled her eyes, but I could tell her heart wasn't in it. She was too wiped out. "I have another three upcoming events to promote and a restaurant opening to put together. Though that's not happening until late July…"

"Take care of *you*," I urged, massaging her shoulders. It was gratifying to see her eyes close, to hear the sigh she released. I could do something, any little thing, to help her, and my heart swelled at the knowledge.

I was dangerously close to being back to where I started. Only I wasn't a kid anymore, in love with the prettiest, smartest, most exciting girl he ever met.

Though she was still all those things, that hadn't changed.

"Are you going to dinner with everybody?" she asked, opening her eyes again. Ari had invited everyone out to a steakhouse on Greenwich Street as a kick-off to the weekend's festivities.

I shook my head. "No, I thought I might hang around and make sure you didn't need anything." She quirked an eyebrow, suspicious, and I had to chuckle at how easily she saw through me. "All right, I asked around and found out you already backed out of dinner to get things done up here. I thought I could come up and help you."

She looked more skeptical than ever, though a tiny smirk stirred the corners of her mouth. "Why do I get the feeling there's a trade-off somewhere?"

"You have so little faith in me," I grumbled, shaking my head. "I'm disappointed."

"So you didn't come up here hoping you'd get laid in exchange for helping me fold place cards?"

"Is that what I'll have to do?" I countered, eyeing the stack of cards again. Funny how much bigger it seemed now.

"How about I order dinner for us?" she suggested, her arms looping around my waist as if I could resist when she pulled me closer. "We can eat and work as long as you promise to keep your fingers clean so you don't smudge the cards."

"There are plenty of things I'd love to do with my fingers that don't involve food."

She placed firm hands against my chest, shaking her head. "Not this close to the wedding, Evan. Work first. Play later."

Who was I to argue?

～

"Is it wrong that I'm hungry again?"

Valentina snorted, her head leaving my shoulder so she could smile sleepily at me. "You worked up an appetite."

I sure as hell had. "It must have been all that folding."

She nudged me, groaning at my terrible joke. "Or maybe the way you folded me like a pretzel."

"Sure. I guess that counts too." I couldn't remember the last time I was this relaxed. The bed was insanely comfortable, the mattress molding itself to my body, the pillow cradling my head. Between that and the woman whose naked body was draped over mine, life was looking pretty good.

"I should book a stay here for myself," she mumbled, stretching like a cat before rolling onto her back. The sheet was down around her waist, letting me admire her perfect, round tits. It was borderline pathetic, the way I turned into a hormonal teenage boy around her.

"What do you do to relax?" I rolled onto my side, trying to ignore her gorgeous tits in favor of holding an actual conversation.

I genuinely wanted to know. She had pretty much ignored me for close to a decade.

"Relax? What's that?" Her laughter was hollow.

"I know you take classes, right? Like, dance or whatever?"

"You remember that?" She laughed softly and chagrined like she was the butt of the joke. "Gosh, I haven't done that in years. There just never seems to be enough time."

"You're always taking care of everybody else." She scoffed gently, which made me double down. "Like when you organized that trip to Vermont so we could all go skiing. You didn't have to do that. But you went out of your way to make sure everybody had a good time, and all the bases were covered."

"Everybody's forgotten about that by now." She sighed, toying with the hem of the sheet like it was suddenly so fascinating. It always made her uncomfortable being praised, which struck me as ironic since so many things about her were praiseworthy.

"I didn't forget." Her eyes dragged up to meet mine, and I was lost in them for a moment too long. Time to take this in a different direction. "Hell, tell me you still go to the carousel in Central Park when you feel overstressed. Do you ever go there anymore?"

She took a deep breath, which she released slowly,

staring up at the ceiling. The way a person sighed after hearing a question they didn't want to answer. "I'm pretty tired," she announced. "I think I need to get to sleep. We have a long weekend ahead of us."

Dammit. When would she stop doing this? "Why are you shutting me down?" I asked. I might have been taking my life in my hands, but I could only go through so much of this hot-and-cold, back-and-forth bullshit.

Here we were, naked in bed, about as vulnerable as two people could be together. All it took was a simple question about something I knew she used to like to do when life got to be too much, and she shut down.

"I'm exhausted, Evan. I barely have it in me to speak, and I have a chock-full schedule from now through Sunday night. What is so wrong with me wanting to get some sleep? Considering you keep telling me to rest."

This was pointless. I couldn't tell what bothered me more. Not knowing what I did to make her go cold or knowing she wouldn't tell me no matter how I tried to get it out of her. "All right. I see your point. I'm going to crash here until morning if that's cool."

Why? I could've left and probably should have. Something wouldn't let me leave her now when she was like this. Instinctively, I felt she needed me, no matter how she pretended otherwise.

"Fine with me." If only she didn't sound so disinterested. What the fuck did I say this time? It was enough to make me wonder if I wanted to stay.

There was no falling asleep right away. I was too busy staring at her back once she rolled away from me, curling in a ball. Protecting herself. From what? Was this all about what happened way back when? If I didn't know for sure we would end up fighting all night with a full day ahead of us tomorrow, I would have asked. I really would have.

There would be time for that after.

We would clear the air once and for all.

The room had been quiet for a long time before the slightest whisper broke the silence. If I'd been asleep, I would've missed it. "I still go there sometimes," she whispered, pulling the duvet up over her shoulder. Whether she thought I was asleep or not, I didn't know. I could only wonder why she wouldn't admit that earlier.

Why did she feel like she had to hide?

"**A**re you sure it's all right for me to go out today?" I turned to Bianca, chewing my lip, torn between a sense of duty to her and wanting to participate in the day for Rose's sake. I had already missed most of her shower and had walked out early on her engagement party. I sort of owed her one event where she would get my attention.

That didn't make it any easier to leave Bianca holding the bag the day before the wedding. It was one thing to have my nails done and a facial yesterday, but the day before the wedding would inevitably bring last-minute issues and small fires that would need to be put out.

She stuck her tablet stylus through her high ponytail before taking me by the shoulders and turning me in place until I faced the front courtyard of the hotel, where a pair of stretch limousines waited to take Rose's wedding party—all of our moms and a few of her other friends—out to the lake that sat nestled between Evan's country club and golf course. I was the lone straggler, practically shifting my weight from one foot to the other, torn over doing the right thing.

"You look absolutely adorable," Bianca pointed out, eyeing my navy-and-white striped top and white pants. I had gone all in on the nautical theme. "You are not going to waste looking this cute on a day spent following florists around a ballroom. I've got this. Go enjoy yourself before I have to tie you up and shove you in the damn limousine."

"Ouch. Fine," I grumbled, slinging a straw bag over my shoulder and taking a deep breath. I had to learn when to step back. While I'd never considered myself a control freak, this wedding was starting to make me reconsider.

"Go," Bianca ordered behind me when I didn't leave fast enough for her. "I'm going to start thinking you don't trust me."

Nothing could've been further from the truth, and that was what got my feet moving. Aria poked her head out through the open window of the second limo when she caught my approach. "Finally! Let's go!"

"Are you always this impatient?" I asked my twin, who'd had her formally amethyst locks tinged a darker shade of blue yesterday. They shone in the sun before she ducked back into the vehicle, where I joined her a moment later. Sienna wasted no time handing me a mimosa.

"You look like you could use a drink," she announced, raising her glass to me. "Let's get this party started!"

"As much as we can party with our moms around," I pointed out, laughing warmly.

Rose snickered, holding a cup of what looked like lemonade. She'd graduated from ginger ale. "Let's be honest. I wouldn't be partying anyway," she reminded us. I wondered if she was consciously aware of the way her hand drifted to her belly, which was still mostly flat.

"How are you feeling?" I asked, sipping my mimosa and settling back against the leather seat. Sienna was right. I did need this.

"Fantastic. I finally turned a corner, thank God." She smiled brilliantly, patting her belly. "I keep telling this kid to give me another couple of days before they decide to start showing themselves, and we'll be all set."

She felt good. That was a good thing. My pulse doubled just the same, and a sick sensation twisted my insides. I'd felt good that awful morning, hadn't I? For the first time in weeks. But everything wasn't okay. It was the exact opposite when I'd started bleeding.

"Don't worry," Aria joked. "If you have a little bit of a tummy in any of your wedding photos, you can just say you ate too much cake."

I tried to laugh with everyone, but it was hollow, half-hearted. I barely heard any of them, their voices blending together in a wall of noise while I consciously forced myself to breathe more slowly. Rose was healthy, the baby was fine, she had gone for a checkup earlier in the week, and the doctor confirmed everything was going according to schedule. My story was not her story. There was nothing to be afraid of.

That didn't mean I could relax. I spent the day only half aware of everything going on around me. "Too distracted with work to have any fun," Mom declared once we were out on the boat, and I didn't bother correcting her. It was safer not to.

~

"OH, MY GOD. THESE ARE GORGEOUS." I looked at Aria and Sienna, both of whom gazed down at the velvet boxes Rose handed to the three of us prior to entering the clubhouse for the rehearsal dinner.

"I was hoping you would all wear them tomorrow," she told us in a shy, sweet voice. "But it's up to you. I'm not going to be a bridezilla about it."

Gazing down at the diamond and sapphire earrings, which glittered stunningly with even the slightest move, I murmured, "Are you kidding? I'd be happy to wear them." The others added their agreement, all of us giggling over how beautiful the earrings were and how generous she was.

"Please, it's the least I can do. You have all been amazing throughout all this craziness. Especially you," Rose added, turning to me with a smile. "You are a gift to everybody who knows you. We are so lucky to have you in our lives, looking after us, making sure we have what we need."

Maybe that's who I'd become, a momma to everyone else when I'd lost the chance.

"Amen." My sister draped an arm around my waist and gave me a little squeeze. "I just wish you would take care of yourself now."

I only offered a weak smile while carefully tucking the velvet box into my purse for safekeeping. I couldn't tell my sister or any of them that it was easier to focus on other people—friends, family, clients—because it meant not having to think too much about myself. That was one thing I had learned through this experience, sort of a wake-up call when it came to the way my mind worked. It was safer to pour my energy into making things perfect for everybody else because they would never be perfect for me.

I was in all kinds of turmoil by the time we gathered together in the country club dining room. Evan was the master of ceremonies, quietly ordering the staff around, offering drinks to the guests, and generally putting everyone at ease. That was a gift he had.

He also had a gift of making my stomach do cartwheels when I set eyes on him. It was that sudden fluttery sensation that made my heart drop in dismay. I cared too much. I had completely forgotten to guard my heart this time around.

And two nights ago, I'd come close to confessing a secret I'd never told anybody. Not even Aria. What was he supposed to do with the fact that I sometimes went to the park and thought about the baby I lost? How I sometimes talked to her in my head while I watched little kids run around, wondering what she would have looked like and what her voice would've sounded like.

It was on the tip of my tongue before I thought twice. He would never understand.

"Here's the bride!" Ari came toward us with his arms outstretched. I had never seen him glowing the way he did when he smiled at his daughter. "I was going to send out a search party if you didn't show up soon."

"I just needed a minute with my girls," Rose explained, kissing his cheek before Colton joined her. She changed right before my eyes, her smile going soft and tender. In another few seconds, she would look like one of those smiley-face emojis with hearts where her eyes should be. If a stranger walked in right now, they would know exactly who this rehearsal dinner was for.

That would never be me.

Lifting my gaze, I found Evan watching me from across the room. We had to maintain appearances in mixed company, and right now, that was a good thing. An excuse to avoid him, to avoid the awkward questions bound to be on his mind and the feelings I hadn't guarded myself against.

Deep, burning regret made my chest ache and tears

burn behind my eyes. I blinked them away, angry with myself for being so weak. My feelings didn't matter now. If I had missed out on the chance to be happy and had trust issues as a result, that was my problem. Not Rose's or anyone else's.

~

IF FEET COULD SIGH in relief, mine would have once I slid out of my strappy sandals in my hotel room. The silence was miraculous after hours spent surrounded by happy, laughing people who insisted on giving countless toasts.

It was past midnight by the time I washed off my makeup. Tomorrow would already be a long day, and it wouldn't get any easier if I didn't get right to bed.

My bridesmaid dress hung over the back of the closet door. I smiled at it in passing, unzipping the dress I'd worn to dinner and pulling on an oversized T-shirt to sleep in.

The following day's itinerary ran through my head as I turned down the bed and grabbed my phone, sliding between the sheets. There was no way I'd be able to sleep without making sure there were no outstanding messages waiting to be answered.

My head touched the pillow before there was a knock at the door. For a second, the idea of pretending I was fast asleep was appealing enough to tempt me, but then there was the chance of missing something important. What if a problem arose and I had ignored it? That was what got me up and across the room so I could peer through the peephole into the hallway.

Except I should've known there was only one person who would knock at my door at this time of night. Evan stood with a hand against the doorjamb, leaning casually, maybe a little drunk after celebrating with the guys. His already sexy hair was tousled, his shirt untucked, and his collar hanging open.

For some reason, what would normally have turned me on only pissed me off. He figured he could show up unannounced, uninvited, and get anything he wanted.

Instead of ignoring him, I opened the door and folded my arms, looking him up and down. Damn his sizzling little smirk as he did the same to me, eyeing my T-shirt. "What are you doing here?" I asked with a roll of my eyes. "It's so late, and I have to be up early. So do you."

"I know." His smirk widened to a knowing smile. I could smell the whiskey on his breath when he leaned in like he was looking for a kiss. "I figured we would sleep better together after a short workout... if you know what I mean."

He entered the room and closed the door behind him, then took me by the waist before I could move beyond his reach. I was in no mood, but it seemed he didn't notice or care.

"What are you doing?" I asked, turning my face away when he leaned down.

"What do you think I'm doing?" He laughed like it was all a game, and I guess to him, it was. That was my fault. I had let him believe I was that easy to sleep with. Touch me the right way, say a few dirty things to turn me on, and I was as good as on my back with my legs in the air.

Resentment bubbled in my chest, searing my insides. Just then, I didn't know who I was angrier with, him or myself, for letting him believe I was so easy to seduce.

"I never said I was in the mood for this tonight," I reminded him, fighting to sound calm and reasonable as I freed myself from his grip. When his hands landed on my hips, I shoved them away, grinding my teeth when he groaned like he was losing something that belonged to him. I did not belong to him. Maybe once upon a time, I thought I'd had, but he shattered that.

"What's the matter this time?" he asked with an exasperated sigh as I went to the bed and sat down. "What did I say that was so wrong?"

"Have you always acted like everything is about you, or am I only noticing it now?"

"For fuck's sake." He threw his hands in the air, shaking his head, muttering all sorts of things I didn't feel like listening to. This was only ever a good time for him. I knew that. He had never made any promises.

I stiffened my spine and lifted my chin. He was not going to coerce me into fucking him tonight or ever again, for that matter. We were never going to have what Colton and Rose found, and I wanted that. I never knew how much until now, with my heart aching and my spirits crumpled. I wanted what they had. Was that so much to ask? *I deserve that.*

With a tight, cheerless smile, I said, "I realize you've gotten used to getting your dick wet whenever we're together, but that's not happening right now."

"Would you at least tell me what's wrong? You've been acting strangely since Thursday night, Friday morning, whatever you want to call it." He waved a hand which he then pointed to the bed. "One minute, we're talking like two normal people, and the next minute, you can't be bothered to say goodnight before turning your back on me. Do you think I'm going to put up with this forever?"

Touching a hand to my chest, I gasped. "Poor thing! How dare I not spread my legs whenever your dick jumps. You are such a heroic figure. Who do you think will play you in the movie about your life?"

"Oh, fuck off," he scoffed, sneering down at me. Incredible how quickly his attitude changed when sex was off the table. He backed away, shaking his head. "You want to be childish, be my guest. I don't have to waste my time witnessing it."

"That's right..." I laughed as he headed for the door, "... I wouldn't want to waste your precious time. I forgot your life is so much more important than mine and always has been."

"What does that mean?" He turned around in the doorway, which his broad shoulders almost filled.

"Why don't you think about it for a little bit?" I asked, folding my arms as I marched toward him. "You're a grown-up. I shouldn't have to spell it out for you."

I tried to close the door on him, but he was too fast, shoving a hand up to hold it partly open. "Are you ever going to get tired of shutting me out whenever you get a little bit uncomfortable?"

For some reason, out of everything that had happened between us, that struck me as hilarious, if not a little sad. "Look who's talking. The man who washed his hands of me the second things got complicated."

There was no way that surprised him. He had to know I would throw it in his face one day. Or was he truly as self-absorbed as I had once believed and convinced myself to forget?

After a moment or two of sputtering on his part, I shook my head in disappointment. "Go take a cold shower," I muttered, taking a second to watch confusion play over his chiseled features before I closed the door between us.

This time, it would have to stay closed. No matter how it hurt, no matter how I wished otherwise.

We were over.

We'd been over for a long, long time.

16

EVAN

"This is it. Are you ready?"

Colton looked my way in the mirror while adjusting his necktie for maybe the tenth time. He wouldn't have admitted it out loud, but he was nervous. I had seen enough grooms in my country clubs to recognize it at first glance. Trying like hell to look confident, since who hadn't heard countless jokes their entire life about grooms getting cold feet and having second thoughts? He didn't want to be one of them, and I couldn't blame him. We both had too much pride.

At least, I thought I had. A certain bridesmaid I had yet to see today made me think otherwise.

"I'm as ready as I'll ever be," he told me, turning away from the mirror in the private dressing room attached to my office. Being the boss had its perks, and I needed to look fresh no matter what the day brought.

Lucian and Noah were already downstairs, greeting guests as they arrived. The ceremony was due to begin in twenty minutes, meaning we'd have to head down shortly. Guests would want to see the groom before the wedding.

"You've got a lot of people down there rooting for the two of you," I pointed out. "Are you feeling good about this?"

"Why does it sound like you're trying to convince me not to go through with it?" He was laughing, so I knew he wasn't serious, though I wondered if he was right. Did I sound that way?

"You know that's not how I mean it," I insisted. "You look a little shaky, that's all. I'm not trying to get in your head. I only want to understand."

"I'm not shaky on my choice. Trust me when I tell you that. I've never been more sure of anything in my life." He ran a hand over his carefully combed hair like he wanted to be sure it was in place before adjusting his cuffs and his tie once again. "I'm not worried about Rose. She's the one."

"Are you worried about yourself?" I guessed, and the way he winced told me I hit the bullseye.

"This isn't like me," he said with a sigh, rolling his shoulders like he was trying to loosen them up. "I've never doubted myself for a minute. I know who I am. I know what I want."

"Absolutely. You always have."

"But I'm standing here, waiting to go down there and marry this incredible woman, and I'm wondering if I have what it takes to be everything she needs."

I knew exactly what he meant. "You know I never had much of an example of how to be a good husband or parent," I murmured, and he nodded. "But you did. I'm not saying things were perfect, but you at least had a good example."

"I did," he admitted.

"Here's the thing," I continued when he didn't look convinced. "The fact that you're so worried about being what she needs tells me you're going to bust your ass to give her everything you can because you want to do right by her. I'm no expert, but I think that's a big part of making a good marriage. I know it sounds clumsy," I admitted, laughing at myself. There was a reason I avoided getting into discussions like this.

He blew out a deep breath and shook his head, a grin playing over his mouth. "It doesn't sound clumsy. You make a good point. So long as I don't lose sight of what matters, everything will be fine. I only want her to be happy and never regret this."

"Regret it? She won't. Have you seen the way she looks at you?" I asked. "She's been in love with you since we were kids, and you know it. And that hasn't changed. Everything's going to be fine."

He lifted an eyebrow. "You wouldn't be telling me that just because there's an elaborate party waiting for us, would you?"

We shared a laugh, clapping each other on the back before leaving my office. He walked with his head high, with confidence I hadn't seen from him all day.

It was no surprise the way my thoughts immediately went to Valentina. She made a point last night. I was in no mood to admit it then, but hours spent on my own after she kicked me out of her room had shed new light on my behavior. I was treating her like a warm hole to stick my dick in, and she deserved better than that. I shouldn't have assumed we would sleep together, especially considering the way she treated me in bed on Thursday night. Was it my fault she never wanted to talk about anything? I didn't like being left guessing at what her thoughts or feelings were.

I also didn't like how much I still looked forward to seeing her, the anticipation building as we reached the lobby, immediately swarmed by guests.

The ceremony would take place outside in the garden, which now held rows of chairs draped with swags of roses, hydrangeas, and gardenias. The fragrance was overwhelming once I stepped outside in a navy suit matching those of the other groomsmen. I raised a hand to Miles, who was hanging out with his stepfather, Magnus, and Evelyn. Since Rose had wanted to keep things small and simple when it came to the bridal party, it meant leaving an odd number of groomsmen versus bridesmaids. He had gracefully stepped back, assuring Colton he didn't need to be a groomsman, considering they hadn't known each other for long.

The girls would be in a small room dedicated to the bridal party, and I wondered if Rose was nervous like her soon-to-be husband. One thing I knew and didn't quite understand was how badly I wanted to find Valentina and tell her I was sorry for last night.

There had to be a way for us to work through whatever was between us. Sure, I could've brushed her aside and given up, but that would be a flawed course of action. After all, we would be part of each other's lives for as long as Colton was my best friend, not to mention my friendships with Lucian, Noah, and Miles. There was no escaping each other.

Not that I wanted to escape her.

I couldn't make heads or tails of my feelings, especially the knot squeezing my ribcage whenever I thought of Valentina as I strode out into the garden, greeting the Diamonds, the Blacks, and the Goldsmiths, making small talk while observing everything with a skilled eye. My staff was on their toes, ushering guests to their chairs and handing out sachets of rose petals to throw at the newlyweds once the ceremony ended. I spotted Bianca hurrying around, whispering instructions, cool and collected. Valentina would be proud when she saw her.

With a few minutes to go until the scheduled start of the ceremony, Bianca caught my eye and gave me a nod. That was my signal. "Okay, let's do this," I told Colton, finding him talking with his parents. Grinning at Lourde, I added, "Don't worry. I'll take good care of him." Her eyes shone with unshed tears when she nodded, gulping back her emotion while Barrett squeezed her closer.

We couldn't have asked for a better day. The sky was deep blue without a cloud in sight, the sun warm but not too hot. The emerald lawn spread out gracefully in all directions, and in the distance, the lake sparkled invitingly. A soft breeze stirred the air and carried the fragrance of all those flowers.

Everything was perfect.

The deep satisfaction that realization brought me was unmatched by anything... but Valentina. There she was again, invading my thoughts, owning my awareness even as I fell in place behind my best friend moments before his wedding. Noah and Lucian stood behind me, and for a moment, I couldn't help but look back on everything that led to this. Our friendship, everything we'd been through together as we learned to make our way in the world. I sure as hell never imagined being the best man at one of their weddings, mostly because I never imagined any of us settling down and getting married.

"You've got this," I told Colton a heartbeat before the doors opened, and Sienna appeared on the veranda.

I was fairly sure Noah choked on his tongue at the sight of her in a tasteful peach dress that flowed and rippled in the breeze. She wore a cluster of gardenias behind her ear and carried a small bouquet of cream and peach roses tied with navy ribbon. The shy smile she wore once she spotted Noah left him catching his breath.

"Okay back there?" I whispered, grinning over my shoulder. "I thought the groom was the one who was supposed to lose it."

"Maybe one day you'll understand," he murmured, staring at her as she walked down the white runner spanning the length of the garden. Aria followed her, and a glance at Miles told me he was having the same reaction Noah had. I was pretty sure his intense stare had him holding his breath too.

It was only when Valentina emerged that I understood. I rocked back on my heels before I could stop myself, my eyes glued to her as she walked slowly and gracefully down a handful of stairs, then down the runner. She held her head high like a queen, smiling at her parents once she found them and then again at her aunt and uncle sitting in the front row, close to where we stood.

Look at me.

Look. At. Me.

See me.

It took all of my concentration to keep a straight face when what I wanted was to run to her, to touch and smell her, and take her in my arms.

I was sorry for whatever I did.

I would tell her so.

I would tell her so many things.

My heart skipped a beat when she found me, our eyes meeting for the briefest moment that somehow stretched out for eternity. I had heard people talk about the world standing still. Romantic comedy bullshit, or so I thought. Now, there I was, frozen in time, staring at her.

She broke the spell by looking away, continuing down

the aisle, and standing in place behind where the bride would make her vows.

Rose looked beautiful, stunning, but it was Valentina I couldn't help glancing at as the bride strode toward us on her father's arm. The warm, loving smile she wore went straight to my heart, making it swell to the point of pain. She loved so deeply, with all of her.

Now I understood I wanted that love for myself. Selfish? Absolutely. I had hurt her. I knew it, even if she wouldn't admit it out loud. And I was a goddamn fool for running from that truth for so long. She deserved better than that. All these years, we might've been together, or maybe not, but possibly. There had been something between us, something real, no matter whether we were kids or not at the time.

It was easier to discount it back then, to pretend we were nothing. Compartmentalize what happened between us and shove all the memories back in a box, hidden in the depths of my mind. It meant being able to move on with my life, which, at the moment, didn't seem all that important in the face of everything I had given up on when I gave up on us.

Would I ever have a chance to make it right?

The officiant stepped up to where Colton and Rose took each other's hands. She smiled brilliantly, tears standing in her eyes. "Hi," she whispered to Colton, who barely grunted a response. He was as bowled over by her as I was by Valentina.

What would it be like to be in his place now? If it was Valentina wearing that white dress and veil?

I was getting ahead of myself, not to mention missing my best friend's wedding ceremony.

It didn't matter how many times I told myself to focus. Valentina was all I could think about, along with the second chance we might be able to take advantage of. I didn't know if she wanted it. I didn't know if I would be able to convince her to give me a shot. Lord knows she should steer clear of me, but I had to try. There had to be a way for us to leave the past behind and start again. No matter how challenging she was, no matter how crazy she made me, I would've preferred that to being bored to death by anybody else. She was what I wanted, what I would always want. And I'd been a damn fool for taking so damn long to figure it out.

I hope it's not too late.

17

VALENTINA

While the guests mingled during cocktail hour, Rose stood at the entrance to the ballroom, one hand covering her chest. Her mouth hung wide open, her eyes as big as saucers, and she stared up at the ceiling to admire what half a dozen florist assistants had worked tirelessly to make it a reality. "Oh, my God!" She gasped.

"Do you like it?" I asked, gazing up at the lush floral garlands suspended from the ceiling, like a cascading vertical garden hanging over the head table and dance floor. It was beyond striking, even better than I had imagined it, and much more colorful and vibrant than the inspiration photos I'd shared with the team.

"It's like something out of a fantasy! Like having my reception in some magical garden." Her eyes shone when she turned to me, caught between laughing and crying. "It's perfect!"

"That's all I wanted for you, for everything to be perfect."

She launched herself into my arms, and we laughed, hugging while pleasant chatter filtered through the closed door between us and the guests. I wanted to have this moment with her, to watch her reaction without anybody else around. She had not disappointed me.

"I can't believe how beautiful everything is." She turned in a circle, her arms extended to the sides, laughing. I had never seen her looking this joyful. "It's perfect! No offense, but I had no idea you'd be able to pull this off so well."

"None taken." We headed back out to mingle, and when Bianca caught my eye, I gave her a thumbs-up. She blew out a sigh of relief, and I did the same before we both laughed. It was all a success. If only my personal life could be taken care of so easily.

I couldn't spend the entire day ducking Evan, but I couldn't resist the impulse to do it either. I didn't have it in me to deal with him. It had been a long day after an even longer weekend, and all I wanted was to be able to enjoy it with my family and friends without thinking back on all of the sadness and pain. Just one day.

BUT THEN HE had to throw me those intense, soul-penetrating glances during the ceremony like he was auditioning for the role of 'Most Intense Gaze' in a romantic drama. A gaze so unnerving I had to ignore him for the rest of the ceremony just so I could get through it.

Why did he have to do this now?

Because you let him. It was my fault. I couldn't pretend otherwise. If I hadn't slept with him all these weeks, avoiding the elephant in the room in favor of screwing around, I wouldn't have to avoid his pointed stare whenever we briefly crossed paths.

One good thing was that he seemed to be busy with something or other, with staff members approaching and asking questions that kept him away from me. He frowned before following one of them back to the kitchen, and as much as I didn't want anything to go wrong, there was a very selfish part of me that was relieved to see his back as he walked away.

It wasn't easy keeping my nose out of the business side of things, but Bianca handled things brilliantly. What a shame I couldn't relax and enjoy myself, but then I hadn't been able to relax since the night of the engagement party. Without the wedding ahead of me to focus my attention on, I wouldn't have anything to distract me. Not at this level.

Then I thought, *to hell with it.* I grabbed a glass of champagne from a passing tray. I didn't have to think about it now, and there was a party about to begin.

A party that lasted well into the night after feasting, drinking, toasting, and dancing. Lots of dancing, both inside and beneath the tent covering the second dance floor out on the lawn. More than a few girls walked with their heels in hand, all of them a little drunk, most of them escorted by men just as tipsy as they were. In other words, everybody was having a great time, and I couldn't have been happier. The whole thing was such a success.

If only it hadn't been for Aria coming my way, holding Evan's hand, and practically dragging him behind her. "Would you please dance with this man before the night ends?" she asked, exasperated. "Neither of you have had a damn bit of fun today."

"Who says?" Evan asked before trying to laugh it off. "I'm having a hell of a good time."

"Sure. Helping out in the kitchen when one of the line cooks got hurt. That sounds like a great time." She blew a strand of hair away from her face, a gesture which hinted at how tipsy she was. It was one of her telltale signs.

When I raised my brows, he shrugged. Now I understood why he was walking around without a jacket, his sleeves rolled up almost to his elbows. "These things happen. It wasn't a line cook, though. I was only helping assemble plates and expediting service."

"Stop. You sound so sexy when you talk that way." Aria placed a hand against my lower back and pulled me closer before shoving us both toward the dance floor. "Dance, you two, before I slap you silly."

If I didn't know better, I would've sworn she was onto us. She couldn't be, though, could she? I had bent over backward to keep her from finding out, both now and years ago.

Evan rocked back on his heels, nodding toward the dance floor. "One song won't kill us," he murmured, piercing me with one of those meaningful looks again. I would have to remember to thank my sister for putting me in this awkward position.

Lifting a shoulder, I grunted, "Sure." It was fairly clear my lack of enthusiasm stung him, but it wasn't my job to protect his ego. I was still hurting after last night and so many other things. I could only blame myself as we found an empty spot on the floor when he took me by the hand and pulled me close enough for the scent of him and the feel of him to weaken my resolve.

Not again.

Not this time.

I owed it to myself not to give in. I was a little stiff in his arms but I made it a point to smile like everything was fine. I had done a lot of that over the years. I could plaster on a Hollywood smile at will.

"Everything went off perfectly," I observed instead of thinking about the feel of his strong hand wrapped around mine. "We made a good team. You'll be bombarded with events after this."

There was a trio of photographers around, plus an entire video team. Content would hit social media within a matter of days, and brides-to-be everywhere would drool over the lavish celebration.

He only grunted like he agreed. "Listen." His voice was barely loud enough for me to hear over the music. "I know I fucked up. It was wrong of me to make assumptions last night or ever. I want to make it up to you."

"You don't have to make anything up to me." How easily that rolled off my tongue. The opposite was true. There was a lot he owed me, but how could I blame him for not realizing it since I had never been honest?

Why was it so easy to look back now and see my mistakes so clearly? Where was all that brilliant insight years ago? Or, hell, months ago? Who did I think I was kidding, telling myself I could handle this when there were so many things left unsaid?

"I feel like I do," he insisted. He lowered his head, making a shiver run through me when his breath touched my ear. "How about we go away for a little while? Just the two of us. It doesn't have to be extravagant... only a way to take a break together. There's so much I want to clear up with you. I would love to start again if you would only give me the chance."

What the hell was I hearing?

More than that. How the hell was I supposed to keep my heart from exploding? My stupid, treacherous heart was determined to betray me again. Urging me to throw away the entire past and all of the betrayal and loneliness in favor of something shiny and new. A turd could be polished to hell and back, but that wouldn't change the fact it was shit.

"Ladies and gentlemen." Bianca's smooth voice filled the air when the music faded. She was standing in front of the band, holding a microphone. "The new Mr. and Mrs. Colton Black would like to invite you out to the garden for the evening's big finale."

Evan and I stilled now that the music was over. There was a general hum of excitement around us as people started leaving the floor, getting up from their tables, and heading out to watch the fireworks scheduled a few minutes from now.

"What do you say?" he murmured, wearing a hopeful yet apprehensive smile. "Will you run away with me for a little while?"

I hated how much I wanted to. More than anything, I hated myself for being weak enough that his offer actually sounded good. I hated myself for wanting him the way I did. I hated him for making me want him when all he'd ever done was leave me hanging after he had his fun.

There was no hope of expressing all of that and so much more. Not here, not now. "I have to go," I decided.

To hell with how it looked.

To hell with everything and everybody.

Who was I kidding, thinking I could handle this?

I would die if I didn't get out. My chest was too tight to breathe, my heart pounding sickeningly. A cold sweat broke out over my skin as I made my way off the dance floor and across the ballroom, going against the flow of traffic. "Valentina. Wait." All Evan's soft urging did was make me move faster since it was him I needed to get away from.

The hotel.

I needed to get back to the hotel to get my things and go home, to lock myself away until the rest of the world left me the hell alone. That was all I wanted, to be left alone. It was all too much, and I couldn't witness another moment of happiness that would never be mine. Not without resenting the hell out of the people I loved.

"Valentina!" Evan caught up to me in the front courtyard, where I took deep breaths in a desperate attempt to loosen my chest while requesting an Uber rather than wait for the shuttle back to the hotel.

"I don't want to see you right now." I managed to get the words out without getting sick. My heart raced out of control, hard and fast enough to scare me a little. "I have to get back to the hotel. I feel sick."

"If you feel sick, why don't you go up to my office and lie down on the couch?"

A scream rose in my throat and threatened to tear its way free. The only thing stopping me was knowing the trouble I would cause. "No, it's better if I go, please. Just believe me, all right? Get back in there before anybody thinks there's something wrong."

"There's obviously something wrong. Goddammit, will you talk to me?" he whispered fiercely, standing close enough to my back that I could feel his warmth and smell his cologne even over the thick fragrance of the flowers in my hair.

"I have nothing to say to you," I whispered, willing the car to get here. "Can you just accept that and let it go?"

"Stop lying."

He was begging for a high heel through his eye, and lucky I was one of the few girls who hadn't taken their shoes off yet. "Oh? I'm a liar now? That's what you think about me?"

"Don't do that." He snarled. "Don't twist this around. You've been hot and cold, up and down for weeks with no explanation."

Don't do this. Not here, not now. You'll regret it forever. I knew the voice in my head was right. I would regret unloading everything on him tonight when the celebration we worked so hard to put together was wrapping up. The bride and groom were probably posing for photos yards from where we stood.

I might have been able to hold it together if he hadn't asked one final question. "When are you going to get tired of running away?"

That was what did it. The accusation that broke my already precarious hold on myself. To hell with regret. I already had more than enough of it anyway. What was a little more heaped on the pile?

I turned slowly, glaring up at him. He had the nerve to look confused. Somehow, that was worse than anything else that he could still look confused. "You are priceless," I gritted out through clenched teeth. "Standing there, accusing me of running away. What did you do when I told you I was pregnant? Did you offer to talk it out with me? Did you ask what I wanted to do about the baby? Did you even think about it as a baby? Did you think about me at all?"

"Wait a second." What a big surprise, the way he wanted to backtrack. "Maybe this isn't the best place—"

Bitterness stiffened my spine. Finally, I had him shrinking under the weight of something I had carried for a decade. "Why not? You were so damn determined to interrogate me only a few moments ago. What's changed, Evan? Can't you handle the truth?"

His face darkened before he lowered his brow, his lip lifting in a sneer. "Maybe I could have handled it if you had brought it up another time instead of throwing it at me now."

"Right." I snapped my fingers, shrugging. "I forgot. You

want to hear things like this when it's convenient for you. That's not how things work. You don't get to use being surprised as an excuse either. Do you think I was prepared for anything that happened back then? Do you think I enjoyed being left on my own? You went to Harvard and didn't look back. You never even called to see how I was feeling," I reminded him, spitting out the words, reveling in how good it felt to get everything off my chest. No, it wasn't the right time or place, but I could not be bothered to give a fuck. I had waited too long.

"I wanted to, Val—"

"Oh, congratulations. *You wanted to.* You're such a fucking hero."

His bewildered gaze hardened before he took another step closer to me, our toes touching, his breath hot on my face. "Tell me something. Why the fuck have you been keeping all of this to yourself all this time? You had ten years to come at me with this."

"It didn't matter so much until..." My voice died, my throat closing up.

"Until what?" His eyes darted over my face. "Why couldn't you tell me? You had every opportunity. We could've worked this out."

"How did I know I was supposed to trust you? How could I make myself believe you wouldn't run away again?" My voice trembled, but I pushed through, determined to get it all out once and for all. "And what the hell difference does it make anyway? This changes nothing. What's done is done. You broke my heart, and nothing is ever going to change that."

His face fell, a breath bursting out of him like he got kicked. "Valentina..."

"I loved you," I told him. To hell with pride, to hell with

consequences. What did any of it matter anymore? I didn't even care that I would have to face him after this since our lives were so inextricably connected. Tears filled my eyes, and my voice shook, but I had to get it out. "I loved you, and you let me down, and I can't believe you would expect me to forget all of that and move on with you when you never even bothered to apologize. And don't tell me you didn't know there was something to apologize for," I added before he could say exactly that. "You left, and you wrote me off, and you have had ten years to make it right. You didn't want to. I get it. But don't act like your change of heart means a damn thing because it doesn't."

A red sedan pulled up in the courtyard and flashed its lights. I checked the plate against the information in the app to confirm. "That's my ride."

"You're still leaving? Now?" He sounded incredulous.

"That's typically what a person does when they get in the car," I called out, my heels crunching on the gravel as I headed for a car that was now my salvation. I was shaking from head to toe, my stomach churning, tears nearly blinding me.

"Running isn't going to do anything," he reminded me, hot on my heels.

"It seems like it always helped you," I retorted. He tried to keep me from opening the back door, but one look at my tear-stained face seemed to take the fight out of him. He fell back a step, his face going slack. "Enjoy the rest of the night," I whispered before climbing into the back seat.

"I'm sorry." He spread his arms in a helpless shrug. "That's all I can say. I'm sorry."

"See? It wasn't so hard to say that, after all." I didn't give a shit about his sorrow or his regret as I closed the door. He only apologized when it was convenient for him.

"Everything all right, Miss?" My driver asked, eyeing me in the mirror.

"As long as you get me out of here," I replied, staring down at my phone rather than glancing at Evan. I released a shuddering sigh as we rolled away from the country club, and before we turned out onto the road, a brilliant burst of color lit the night sky. I twisted in my seat, watching the blue, red, and golden explosions. It was spectacular, the perfect end to a perfect evening.

Not for me, though. I could barely see, thanks to the tears in my eyes as I typed a text to Bianca.

Me: *You were such a rock star this weekend. Thank you for everything. I am officially giving you the coming week off. No excuses, no arguments. I am going to take a little time to myself as well. There's nothing that can't wait until next week. We both have more than earned a little break. Enjoy it.*

What was the point of owning my own business if I couldn't retreat for a little while when it felt like my whole world was tumbling down?

Dropping the phone in my lap, I covered my face with my hands, sobbing quietly in the back seat of a stranger's car while the world lit up all around me. That was how I'd been for so long. Aware of the beauty and life surrounding me but unable to enjoy it.

18

EVAN

"We're going to need to bring in a second event coordinator if this keeps up." Serena pinched the bridge of her nose, rubbing it like she was trying to ward off a headache. "I mean, I'm not complaining that we have all these new requests after the wedding, but I don't know that we have enough manpower to cover all of it."

"I'll have to look into that," I agreed, though my heart wasn't in it. "Things are going to be pretty busy going forward."

"You know, those properties you were looking at in Rhode Island and that second place in Cape Cod are still on the market," she pointed out, sort of playful. "I know you were thinking about making an offer. With all this new business coming in, nothing's holding you back now. You could take your empire as big as you want so long as you promise to keep me on in some capacity."

I offered a sincere, if weary, grin. "Believe me. There are a lot of things I could do without, but you are not one of them."

My phone buzzed with a text, and the sight of Aria's name on the screen pushed everything out of the way for now. I turned back to my Mac, where Serena chatted with me over Zoom. "I need to get going. I have another meeting here in town. When I'm back in the office, we'll go over all these new inquiries."

"And the information on those other properties?"

"We'll see." It was almost unthinkable but no less true. I could hardly remember why it had ever seemed so important, having a certain number of properties under my belt by the time I turned thirty.

What difference would it make? Would I be any happier? Would it fill some void in my life?

I grabbed my phone and pulled up Aria's text like it was a life jacket on a stormy sea. It had been a few hours since I reached out to ask about Valentina, who'd been completely MIA since the wedding. By Friday morning, I had decided enough was enough. I needed answers. If I couldn't get my response from her, Aria seemed like the natural person to turn to.

Aria: *Meet me at the café in the lobby of my building. I'll be down there in fifteen.*

Thank fuck. I was afraid for a minute there she would stonewall me the way her sister had. It had been a long, ugly five days since Valentina handed me my ass outside the country club. She hadn't said anything I didn't need to hear. That didn't make the memory easier to bear or the wounds easier to deal with.

I'd hurt her so much worse than I had ever imagined. I could hardly stand to look at myself in the mirror, knowing she had loved me, and I broke her heart.

She had never told me that. There was so much I never knew.

I wasted no time getting across town to the apartment building on Central Park West, where Aria and Miles had been living there together for a couple of months.

The café off the lobby was busy, full of customers craving their caffeine fix. Aria hadn't come down yet, so I picked up a cup of black coffee for me and an oat milk latte for her after hearing her order one the morning after the wedding. She was still nowhere around by the time I took a seat at a two-top by the window overlooking the street.

Valentina would hate knowing I went to her sister for help. Nobody wanted to know the people in their life went behind their backs to talk about them. She had to understand this was all the result of caring so damn much about her. I lived and breathed Valentina since the engagement party. Nearly every fucking, waking moment was all her.

And if she refused to? Well, that would be par for the course.

A head full of blue hair bobbed on the other side of a line of customers, and a moment later, Aria broke through, spotting me at the far end of the room. The worry lines between her delicate brows told an entire story before she reached the table.

"Thanks for coming down to talk to me," I offered. "I got you an oat milk latte if you're interested."

"Oh, thanks. That was thoughtful." She dropped into the chair across from mine and opened the lid of her cup. "So. My sister. You're not the only one she's basically shut out of her life all week. I get, like, one-word texts from her, and only when I ask her to let me know she's still alive."

My heart sank. There I was, hoping I was the only one she had blocked out. "It's my fault. She's mad at me. I made a huge mistake."

"You've made mistakes before," she pointed out, smirking. "What's so different this time?"

Her smirk faded as silence unfurled between us. The longer it took me to come up with a reasonable explanation for what had gone down, the more serious she became. "What did you do?" she eventually asked in a whisper, the way a person asked a question whose answer they weren't sure they wanted to hear.

If there was one conclusion I'd come to, it was how pointless denial was. What had I gained from pretending not to understand how traumatic Valentina's experience must've been? Like a coward, I had told myself if she didn't bring it up, I didn't need to either. Obviously, it had eaten away at her, not to mention eating away at anything we might have had together.

Still, I couldn't find the words, and I didn't want to betray Valentina worse than I already had. Aria made it easy for me. She looked down at her cup, turning it in place and tapping her fingers against the cardboard. "You were the father, weren't you?" she asked, and the sudden question took my breath away. "Don't pretend you don't know what I'm talking about because I think you do. I don't feel like being insulted with a lie."

Jumping right into it, were we? That was fine. We needed to. Valentina needed us to. "Yeah. It was me."

Head bobbing slowly, she murmured, "I've noticed the way she's acted around you lately, deliberately avoiding contact when we're all together. She ran from you like the plague throughout the reception. I was watching."

"Which was why you bullied us into dancing together?"

Her gaze met mine before darting away, cheeks going pink. "So you started up again. I thought you might have been hiding something. Now that I know you were the baby's father, I have to admit, none of this makes any more sense than it did before."

"I didn't know you knew about the baby." How completely insane it was, sitting there, opening up this way. I had never talked about the baby after the phone call from Valentina the morning after the miscarriage.

"She wouldn't have told me if I didn't walk in on her almost passed out on the bathroom floor that night." I heard it all in her voice. How terrifying that must have been for her, for both of them.

"Oh, Jesus," I muttered, gripped by nausea.

"She wouldn't tell me who the father was, and I've wondered through the years. It's not like I sat around thinking about it all the time, but every now and then, I would catch her, you know... staring at a baby or a pregnant woman a little too closely. But you know how she is," she concluded with a sigh. "God forbid anybody thinks she is less than totally fine."

Guilt plagued me, wrapping its way around my throat in a chokehold. "I should have known she wasn't fine."

"You're right. You should've known." Her nose wrinkled, eyes crinkling at the corners when she winced. "Sorry. You couldn't have known. We were kids. Both of you did the best you could."

"That's not true." Her features pinched together like she was in pain, but I shook my head anyway. "I could have done better. I should have done more. I took the easy way out and pretended it was for the best. Hell, I saw how upset she got the night of the engagement party when Colton announced Rose's pregnancy. I could've stepped up then, but I told myself too much time had passed. I've been making excuses all these years, now more than ever. I don't deserve understanding or sympathy."

"I appreciate your honesty." With her elbows on the table, she leaned in, hitting me with a hard stare. "She changed after that. I don't know if you noticed it because you always spent more time with the guys. She's my twin. She's the other half of me. I felt her pulling away and... I don't know. Getting harder. That natural light she had... remember it?"

"I sure as hell do." The memory of the day we met was as sharp and clear as ever. She had drawn me to her light like a moth to a flame.

"It seems like everything after that was forced. She's still bright and amazing, but she has to work at it. She may have recovered physically, but emotionally?" Shaking her head, she concluded, "She's never been the same."

I saw it all so clearly now that Aria laid it out that way. "What can I do? She hates me. She should, she has every right to. I thought maybe we could move forward, start again, but she may as well have spat in my face."

"Maybe that's where you need to leave things," she suggested in a soft voice. "Some things aren't meant to be. If being with you is hurting her, it might be for the best to let her go."

She made sense, but then certain things didn't follow logic, and this was one of them. "We had something real. I felt it again when we were together these past weeks. That natural connection. If I hadn't been such an ignorant coward, we wouldn't be having this conversation now."

Her mouth pursed thoughtfully as she sat back, picking up her cup and taking a sip. "You're going to try to get her back, aren't you?" she asked with a sigh.

"I have to. I can't let her go without trying." Gazing toward the park across the street, an idea came to mind. "And I might know how to find her."

19

VALENTINA

The breeze stirred my hair as I sat with an iced coffee on my usual bench. The weather was almost too perfect, which meant there were people everywhere, hanging out on blankets spread across the emerald grass, walking dogs, and jogging. Kids shouted and laughed while waiting in line for the carousel. Somebody was playing music somewhere, and the happy beat left me swinging my foot after I crossed my legs.

I wouldn't say this out loud to anybody since I knew how it sounded, but there were times when I felt more at home on a bench across from the Central Park carousel than anywhere else.

Sometimes, I liked it better here during gloomy weather. I would put on my raincoat and sit here alone with my thoughts and talk to the baby who only existed in my head. Good thing I didn't feel super low today. Troubled, torn, but not super low. The sight and sound of so many other people enjoying a beautiful day didn't feel like a blade to the heart the way it sometimes did.

Spotting a little girl with dark brown pigtails, I thought,

She looks like I've imagined you would look if you ever had the chance. You would be much bigger than her now, almost ten years old. What would you like to do? What would you be good at? I wonder all the time. Would you be creative? Artsy? Would you play an instrument, or would you rather play sports? Not that you would've had to choose. I would have encouraged you to do anything you wanted. No limits.

Before Rose announced her pregnancy, it had been a long time since I came here to talk to Chloe. That was what I'd named her in my head. My beautiful girl. *I didn't forget you. I will never forget you. But sometimes... it's easier to carry you quietly in my heart and try to move on. I thought I had, really, I did. I was wrong.*

I needed to. There was no way I could live otherwise.

The icy coffee was a treat, cooling on a warm afternoon. I sipped it, sighing, wondering where to start putting this behind me. Evan, our past, our present. How could I ever move on when I'd never be able to avoid him for long? How could I have been so careless, getting involved with him again?

The week since the wedding hadn't done much to ease the burning, raging anger. It wasn't him I was angry at—not anymore. It was me. I knew better. That hadn't stopped me. I was a child who couldn't be told the flame would burn my skin. I needed to hold my hand over it and find out the hard way.

What was it that caught my attention? Was it the scent of cologne I would know anywhere floating my way on the breeze? No, I would feel him anywhere, no matter what he was wearing. Something inside me had always been able to sense him.

Taking a deep breath, I turned my head slowly until I found Evan standing a few benches down from where I sat.

He was dressed like so many people walking past in both directions, wearing a T-shirt and jeans, his hands sliding into his pockets once my attention landed on him.

My heart stuttered. Why was it so impossible to let go of him? My blood hummed, and my body went warm, all because he was within my field of vision. Weariness I'd spent a week trying to ignore settled over me like a heavy blanket. What I wouldn't have given if he would only hold me, soothe me, piece me back together.

"What are you doing here?" I asked. I would have stood and might even have walked away if it wasn't for the trembling that spread throughout my body when I saw him coming. But I didn't trust myself to get up from the bench without falling flat on my face.

"I thought I might find you here." He stood yards away, under the shade of a graceful tree, but even at a distance, I recognized the way his eyes shone with what might have been tears. What was this about? "I've come over here the past few days, waiting around, hoping I'd see you."

"You didn't," I deadpanned. "Tell me you're exaggerating."

"I haven't gotten a word out of you in a week. Going to your apartment would've been a waste of time. For all I knew, you would have called the cops. We didn't exactly end things well last weekend." Shrugging, he added, "What else could I do but hope you still came here?"

The idea of him wandering around here, hoping to see me, did funny things to my heart. *Don't do this. For once, don't make it that easy.* "You found me. Congratulations." I crossed my legs, folding my arms, doing everything I could to protect myself. My body was one thing, but my heart? It throbbed with every beat, threatening to burst out of my chest. "I come here to be alone."

"You don't have to be. I could be here with you. I... I want to be with you."

"When it's convenient for you? When I tear you a new one, and you feel like you have to do something to work your way back into my—" A pair of little girls ran past, squealing over something, and I thought twice about my choice of words. This wasn't the place.

"That's not what I'm trying to do." When I sighed, rolling my eyes, he groaned. "I swear. This isn't about that. I made so many mistakes. I always knew I did, and I never had the guts to come clean and tell you everything I was thinking and feeling."

"You still haven't found the guts," I reminded him. Because fuck it, if he was going to invade my privacy this way and think he suddenly understood everything because he found me sitting on a park bench, I was determined to stand my ground. "What are you thinking and feeling? What were you thinking and feeling back then that you couldn't tell me about?"

He looked pained, and I was glad. Let him be. Let him feel a fraction of what I'd carried all this time. "I was... shocked," he gritted out.

He took a step in my direction, then another. When I braced myself, sitting up a straighter, he paused. "I was scared shitless. All of a sudden, I saw every plan I ever had for my life dissolving. I could hear my dad in my head, reminding me how irresponsible I was, telling me I was lucky he could give me a safety net. I didn't want his safety net. And I didn't want your father cutting my balls off for getting his daughter pregnant."

"You never thought to ask me what I wanted to do about the baby," I reminded him. It was like sticking my finger in a wound and wiggling it around, stirring up as much pain as possible, but this was the only way to get through it. After ten years, I wanted to get through it. No, I *needed* to.

"I know. For what it's worth, you didn't give me the chance." He held up a hand when my mouth fell open, shaking his head. "I'm not blaming you. But you did run off before I could fully process the news. You didn't give me a chance, and I punked out and didn't call you because I was sure you didn't want to talk to me. I thought I destroyed everything to the point where I couldn't make it better."

He sat on the bench beside mine, leaning forward with his elbows on his knees, staring at the carousel. "I don't know. I guess it was safer that way too. Easier in the short term. I told myself if you wanted to keep the baby, you would tell me, and we would work it out. Every day that passed, I waited for that call. And then you did call, and you told me..."

I finished for him, "Told you it was all over." The memory of that call was clear, sharp as a knife. "Which I'm sure was a relief."

"I was an eighteen-year-old guy who just found out his life could keep going the way he planned. Of course, it was a relief." He turned to me, and now a tear rolled down his cheek. "And I was too ignorant and immature to imagine what it did to you. I assumed it was a relief for you the way it was for me. You wouldn't have to sacrifice anything either."

As much as I didn't want to accept that, it made sense.

"I've never been great at guessing what people are feeling," he admitted, running a hand across his cheek, catching the tear that had escaped. "And even now, I'm not much better than I was at eighteen. If you had told me what you were thinking and feeling, I would've come back to be with you for as long as you needed. I want you to know that. I *need* you to know that. I know... it's easy for me to say it now..." he scoffed, waving a hand, "... but it's the truth. I would have. I loved you. You were the love of my life, Valentina."

I drew a hitching breath, tears spilling over my lashes. Here we were, sitting in public, blubbering like idiots. Yet we were closer now, fully clothed and sitting feet apart than we had ever been in our most intimate moments. This, right here, was real intimacy. Vulnerability. Sharing what mattered.

"Dammit, I *still* love you." His voice was low but filled with intensity that sent a tingle down my spine and spread certainty through me. "I understand you might never be able to return that love, and I don't blame you. But I'm here now. I'm here for you. If you need help processing things and dealing with your feelings, I want to help in any way I can. You don't have to do it on your own. Not anymore."

Emotion tightened my throat and made my eyes leak again, harder this time. If anyone passing happened to notice us, they would probably think we were breaking up.

"I've felt alone for so long." I brushed a tear away, but it was only followed by another. "And that's partly my fault. I was too proud to tell anybody what happened. I wouldn't have told Aria if she hadn't found me like she did. There's another side of the coin I didn't think about back then. I painted myself into a corner by keeping it all to myself. And I obviously gave you the idea I got over it like it didn't matter."

"I should have known better," he insisted in a voice heavy with sorrow.

"You couldn't have."

"I'm sorry. So sorry." He got up and moved to my bench, giving me space rather than smothering me. "I'll never stop being sorry for everything. All the mistakes, all the time I wasted telling myself what we had back then wasn't real. The lies I fed myself so I could get over you. Get over us. You were so... extraordinary in every way. I couldn't imagine you felt anything real for me."

"Are you kidding?" A laugh burst out of me, and it felt good. "I was crazy about you. When it seemed like you were in a hurry to get away from me at college and I never heard from you, I convinced myself it was stupid to ever fall for you in the first place."

"But you did fall for me?"

The hope in his voice melted what little was left of the ice I tried to build around my heart. Reaching out, I caught what was left of the moisture on his cheek. "Yes. Hard. Completely."

He caught my hand, turning his face toward it to kiss my palm. "And now? Please tell me I don't have to live without you. I don't know if I could handle it. I will do everything, whatever you want, to make sure I never make the mistake of losing you again."

All it took was him opening his eyes and gazing into mine. I never stood a chance, did I? I loved him then. I loved him now. If I hadn't known it before today, all it took was the tears he'd shed to lift the veil from over my eyes. Now, I could see clearly.

"Of course, I love you," I whispered. "You idiot. What do you think?"

He burst out laughing, and before I knew it, I was in his arms where I belonged. Where I could finally set down the burden I'd been carrying long enough that I'd gotten used to it. Breathing was easier without weighing me down.

"I'm never leaving your side." He kissed my cheeks, my forehead, and my nose until I giggled helplessly and hoped nobody was watching too closely. "You're never getting rid of me."

"Who said I wanted to?" I asked, smiling through my happy tears before a kiss said everything I couldn't find the words for.

~

It was dark when we reached my apartment, the day melting in the face of everything we had to say to each other. An afternoon spent strolling Central Park hand in hand had turned into dinner, with neither of us wanting to break the magic we had wound around ourselves.

Now that the truth was out there—our feelings, the past, everything that had been keeping us apart—what happened after we stepped through the door and closed it on the rest of the world was inevitable.

Our bodies crashed together, and like always, I was swept up in the moment—being close to him, touching him, sizzling in the heat of his caress. But there was something more to it now. Something so deep, I was almost afraid of the intensity. I had to fight the urge to hide from him when happy tears filled my eyes.

There was nothing to be afraid of. I knew it when our mouths met and he wrapped his arms around me, pulling me close enough that I could feel his heart pounding away. I knew how he felt because mine thudded so hard it made me dizzy. That could have been the effect of his touch—gentle but full of promise. We had been here before, so many times. Only this time, there was the prospect of forever involved.

"I love you." His breathless whisper in my ear made my tears spill over. We had almost missed this. I locked my arms around his neck and pressed my face against his shoulder, overwhelmed, weak against the power of those words and what they meant.

He loved me.

I was the love of his life.

He was the love of mine.

I didn't have to be afraid anymore. There was something joyful about giving myself to him, melting against him once he backed me against the door, holding me in place with his body so his hands could run all over me.

"I can't wait to do this for a very, very long time." He chuckled softly, finding my mouth again, stroking my tongue with his until I was completely under his spell. I would've done anything he asked. I would have given him anything so long as he never stopped lighting my body and soul on fire with his skillful touch and his deep, searing kisses.

When he started sliding my cardigan over my shoulders, I did the work for him, letting it fall on the floor so he could rain kisses over my bare skin, dropping the straps of my sundress, dragging his lips over my shoulders and across my chest while his hands worked their way up my thighs. His mouth moved lower, his teeth catching the top of the dress and pulling it down, inching it over my breasts until they were bare. My back arched when he molded them in his hands, lifting them to his lips, kissing them almost reverently. The pleasure was just as hot and consuming, but the urgency was gone. In its place was tenderness.

"You're so perfect," he grunted out between laps against my skin. There was nothing for me to do but run my fingers through his hair and lose myself in him as he went lower, finally pulling down my thong to press hot, breathless kisses against my mound.

"And this." His already deep voice dropped in pitch, his breath against my shaved skin driving me wild. "I could live on this."

It was like he wanted to prove himself. The next thing I knew, he draped my right leg over his shoulder and buried his face in my pussy.

"Oh, God, Evan..." The back of my head touched the door. My eyes closed, all of my awareness narrowing down to the place where his tongue touched me. It was unspeakable, the pleasure, so good it almost hurt, so good there was nothing I could do but stand and let him claim every inch of me.

Soon, my needy whimpers were louder than his deep grunts. His tongue worked me to the point I could only hold onto the back of his head as the tension broke, replaced by wave after wave of warm, sweet bliss.

I was still trembling by the time he stood, pulling off his T-shirt and dropping his jeans and boxer briefs to his knees. His rigid cock pressed against my stomach when he leaned close, touching his forehead to mine.

"I love you." He lifted my leg, this time draping it over his hip before driving himself into me all at once. The sensations that had only started to fade came back in full color, even stronger than before. I dug my nails into his firm shoulders before he took my wrists and pinned them above my head, holding me in place as he moved, taking me in slow, deep strokes.

"Mine. Mine always." His dark eyes searched mine as he spoke and filled and stretched me, taking me to the edge. "Say it. Tell me you're mine."

"Yours." With pleasure wiping out almost every conscious thought, that was the one thing that remained. "Yours, always." There was something so right about saying it, about letting go and handing my heart, my life, and my future to him. No more fear. No more regret.

Nothing but the satisfaction of taking him inside me and feeling him lose control one stroke at a time, one kiss at a time. "I'm gonna come," I whispered in his ear, gasping when he responded in a flurry of quick, sharp strokes.

"Come for me. Let me feel you tighten around me," he urged.

It pushed me over the edge before I knew what was happening, my teeth sinking into his shoulder to muffle my scream. I was still gasping in surprise when Evan let go and filled me with a rush of warmth, then almost fell against me.

My fingers ran through his hair while I laughed softly. "Did I wear you out?" I asked, kissing his temple before he lifted his head.

"Not even close." His eyes narrowed, a smirk tugging the corner of his mouth. "Only resting briefly before round two. And three."

"You'd better be careful," I warned while my body tingled at the idea. "I might start getting used to this."

His smile lit my heart. "How do you know that wasn't my plan all along?"

20

EVAN

There were worse ways to start the day than this. In the shower, enveloped by steam, having my dick slowly and eagerly sucked by the woman I loved. Her soft moans blended with my grunts and groans like a symphony only the two of us could write.

I opened my eyes and looked down to watch. Her already dark hair was nearly black, thanks to the water beating down on us. She took me in slow, sensual strokes, hands sliding up and down my chest and abs while her tongue worked magic.

"That's right," I groaned out when she sucked on my swollen head. "It's so good. You are so good at that."

It was like the praise only made her want to work harder. I closed my eyes again, my knees going weak once she started sucking hard enough to hollow her cheeks. Her head bobbed faster, and she moaned again, leaving me hanging on the edge between tension and release.

Which was why, as much as I hated it, I had to pull her away before I came. "You are incredible," I told her, brushing wet hair away from her face before kissing her deeply.

Until she pulled back, anyway, with her eyes twinkling. "How incredible?" The little tease. She loved it, but then so did I. It drove me crazy her taking her tits in her hands and squeezing them while I watched, transfixed.

There was nothing in the world hotter than the sight of her with water running down her skin and her hair trailing over her chest and shoulders.

"Touch yourself for me." I took my dick in hand, slowly fucking my fist while she backed up far enough for the shower spray to cover her. "Use the showerhead," I suggested, grinning when her eyes widened.

"Are you saying you want me to make myself come for you?" she asked in a seductive voice, reaching up to free the detachable head.

"Fuck, yes."

"It probably won't take long." She trained the water against her pussy, closing her eyes. "You know how hot it gets me, having your cock in my mouth."

"My cock loves your mouth." It loved her pussy more, but at that moment, a stream of water massaged her clit. Her eyes closed, her mouth falling open for a long, low moan to fill the air.

"Mmm... that's good..." She sighed, spreading her lips open with one hand, applying the stream directly to her bundle of nerves. I almost forgot to breathe when her head fell back, her tits heaving when her breathing turned sharper in a panting rhythm.

"Get yourself good and hot for me." My fist moved faster, the tingling in my balls intensifying the harder she breathed. "Make sure your pussy is ready for my cock."

"Almost... there..." She whined, straining, the showerhead almost touching her skin when she held it close. "I'm... Evan!"

It was so satisfying to watch her shatter. Her skin flushed, her gorgeous face contorting in complete ecstasy. I couldn't wait any longer. I was getting close as it was and wanted to save every drop for her.

With the showerhead back in place, I turned her to face the tiled wall. She was still moaning and trembling by the time I lined up with her dripping entrance and drove myself deep. Her back arched, hips lifting and letting me sink deeper than before. "Oh, fuck," I whispered, savoring the sensation of the still-spasming muscles massaging me from tip to base.

"Mmm... you feel so good inside me..." She turned her head, hitting me with a look that turned my blood to fire, racing through my veins.

"How does this feel?" I took her harder, faster until our bodies slapped together and sent water flying. Her cries echoed in the steam-filled stall, almost deafening me, but I wouldn't have asked her to quiet down for anything. Instead, I slapped her ass hard enough to make her squeal and push back against me, riding me the way I rode her.

Looking down, I watched myself disappear inside her with every stroke. She fit me like a glove, tighter all the time. "You fuck me so good." She moaned, looking back at me over her shoulder again. "You fill me completely."

In response, I took her by the throat and held her head still so our mouths could meet. There was nothing like this. Controlling her pleasure while mine built, feeling her body's response, knowing only I could take her to this place. Only I ever would.

She was close again, every breath a whimper stifled by my kiss. So tight. So perfect. By the time she clamped down around me, I was seconds away from losing control, so there was no holding on once she began to milk me, writhing and whimpering while a million muscles massaged my shaft.

I followed her, letting the rush overtake me, the tingle at the base of my spine exploding and rippling through my limbs. Complete release. It had only ever been this intense and all-consuming with her.

Once she caught her breath, Valentina pushed away from the wall with a soft laugh. "So much for a quick shower together."

"It always turns out that way, doesn't it?" Not that either of us was complaining. Lazy Sunday mornings were something I had grown to love over the past three months of being together, living in my apartment. Sundays used to be devoted to sleeping off the damage I'd done on Saturday night.

Now, the time I spent in bed was spent with her. Drinking coffee, eating breakfast, catching up on the news or whatever show she had roped me into watching with her. We were learning together how to slow down. Not every moment of every day had to be spent at work.

We also enjoyed lazy brunches with her family and our friends. The first time we showed up holding hands, their jaws hit the floor. Colton and Noah couldn't believe it while the girls squealed like we were a shiny new toy. All except Aria. She was cautious and rightly so. But now she saw how far I'd go to realign the stars for her sister and had come around.

We washed up quickly, turning off the shower and stepping out of the stall. I draped a fluffy robe over her shoulders while she toweled her hair, watching her reflection in the mirror. There was no way I could have expected the sort of satisfaction that warmed my chest in simple moments like this when our eyes met, and she smiled.

"How about going out for something to eat?" I rubbed a towel over my hair before wrapping it around my waist and heading back to the bedroom.

It wasn't until I reached the bed that I noticed she lingered in the doorway. "What's up? Not in the mood for overpriced brunch?" I joked. "You don't like watered-down mimosas all of a sudden?"

The briefest smile touched her lips. "I don't think that would be a good idea." She toyed with the robe's belt, cinched tight around her waist. "There's something I have to tell you."

"Why don't I like the way this is going?" I asked, suspicious. "What is it?"

She took a deep breath and gulped hard before the words tumbled out. "I'm pregnant."

Everything stopped. My heart, my breathing, the world. *Pregnant.* The past and the present overlapped in the most uncanny way. This time, we were different people.

Something in my face must have freaked the hell out of her since the color drained from her cheeks. "Say something," she whispered, wincing.

It was her wide eyes that snapped me back into reality after getting the surprise of my life. "You are?" I crossed the room again, taking her face in my hands, searching for confirmation. "You're sure?"

"I went to the doctor this time to be extra sure," she told me, covering my hands with hers. "Is that okay? I mean, are you happy?"

"No, I'm not happy. I'm elated!" She barely had the time to take a breath before I threw my arms around her, lifting her off her feet and turning her in a circle. "A baby! *Our* baby!" It was the greatest gift she could give me. It was everything. A real, true second chance.

"Thank God." She was laughing and crying as her arms wrapped around my neck. "I was so worried you wouldn't be happy."

"Let me tell you something." I set her on her feet, serious now, looking her straight in the eye so she'd know I meant it. "Here's something I want you to know, now and always. I love you. I want you forever. And I want a family. I want to fill a house with our kids someday."

"Hang on!" She shook her head firmly, laughing through her tears. "Let's not get ahead of ourselves. One thing at a time."

But that was the thing. We had forever. There was nothing in front of us but the rest of our lives, and I planned on spending mine building the sort of future I'd never imagined.

Until now. Until her.

"I love you. God, I fucking love you." It was all I knew as I kissed her again and again, pulling her across the room with me until we ended up back in bed. Her helpless laugh filled the room as I pressed her back against the mattress, devouring her neck, feasting on her sweet skin.

"We just showered," she reminded me as I tugged her robe's belt while she ran her fingers through my wet hair.

"We can shower again," I reminded her while peeling the robe back like I was unwrapping the ultimate gift that was her. A gift to me.

Now, she was working on another gift. This time, I wouldn't take it for granted. Not for a single minute.

EPILOGUE
LUCIAN

"Are you ready?" My father eyed me from the other side of his desk as he stood and buttoned his suit jacket. Most men his age, sitting at the head of a media empire, might consider backing off a little, enjoying life in his mid-sixties, spending some of the wealth he'd amassed, not that he could hope to spend it all.

Instead, he was as active and involved in Diamond Media as he'd ever been, leaving me wondering if he ever planned to retire. Not that I was chomping at the bit to take his place. It would've been nice to have a little warning, was all, considering I was the reluctant heir apparent.

This was hardly the first buyout Dad had masterminded over the decades after he'd taken my grandfather's place. It was, however, the first I'd taken part in as the corporation's new Vice President of Digital Media. We'd recently completed the purchase of a dying brand, a dinosaur helmed by stubborn old men who refused to keep up with the times. It would be my task to fold their employees in with our own.

And to cut loose anybody who couldn't hack it.

I had to be merciless. This was business, nothing personal.

I nodded firmly, following close behind him as we strode out of his corner office and down the hall to the large conference room where the former employees of Jones Media, Inc. sat in chairs arranged in rows, facing the screen where a welcome presentation would play. I'd prepared a few words, after which point Dad would wrap things up.

A nervous, tense energy hummed in the air as we entered the room, our every move followed by dozens of pairs of eyes—mistrusting, anxious. No doubt they wanted to make a good impression and prove why they were necessary to the company. Their livelihoods depended on it.

"Oh, Lucian. Can I have a moment?" Dad motioned for me to follow him to the far corner of the room, where a young woman stood with her back to the wall, her attention focused on her phone. There were a handful of empty chairs among those already taken, but she had decided to stand. Her rigid posture drew my interest, but it was a curtain of icy-blonde hair that held my attention, stirring my memory. Why? It was like having a word on the tip of my tongue, just out of reach. I knew her from somewhere.

Dad cleared his throat. "Ivy St. James?"

Her head snapped up, the phone finding her pocket as she offered a tight, professional smile. It was when her steely gray eyes met mine that worlds collided. I knew her. Weeks had passed since the night we spent in my hotel room, but she was not the sort of woman whose face faded to nothing the morning after.

Considering the way her fair cheeks flushed, she recognized me too. I'd hope so. The woman had raked the hell out of my back in the hours after Colton's wedding.

Dad was completely unaware, shaking her hand. "I wanted to introduce you to my son, Lucian Diamond. You two will be working closely together in the coming weeks as we blend our two families together."

It wouldn't be the first time we'd worked together, though we hadn't exactly been clothed at the time. To think fate threw us together again. For once, I was glad to run into a one-night stand after the fact.

Until Dad's choice of words sank into my overheated mind. "We'll be working closely together?" I asked, looking from her to my father. "How so?" And why the hell hadn't he mentioned her before now?

"Ivy here was Vice President of Digital Media at Jones," he explained.

"For the six months we began developing a digital brand before the buyout," she added, staring at me as I stared at her. Yes, she definitely remembered.

What mattered more was the implication of her job title. "We need two VPs?" I asked Dad, grinding my teeth in a parody of a smile.

"Ivy will assist you in learning the ropes of the position..." he explained. "Since she has a bit more experience. And her familiarity with the people we brought in will help us determine how to put their talents to use."

What a crock of shit. He wanted her around to babysit me. He didn't trust me to do this on my own. Why else would he keep her around?

I'd have the pleasure of knowing she was looking over my shoulder, possibly reporting to Dad on whether I could handle the position. For all I knew, she was already planning to take the job for herself. Any growing hope of continuing what we'd started at the wedding died a quick death then and there.

"I look forward to working with you, Mr. Diamond," she offered, extending a hand to shake mine.

When I clasped it, I had the feeling I was about to begin the fight of my life.

READ LUCIAN DIAMONDS STORY NEXT…

Delicious Tropes you can expect:
Enemies to Lovers, Forced Proximity in workplace, One-bed Trope & Witty Banter, Spicy encounters

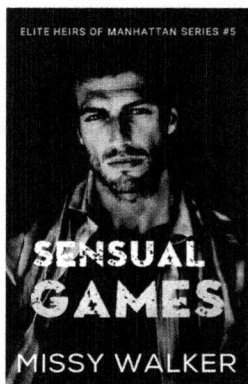

Preorder SENSUAL GAMES today!

21

BONUS SCENE

Don't want to let Evan and Valentina go just yet?

Grab the FREE bonus scene here:
https://dl.bookfunnel.com/kkk6v9nzaa

ALSO BY MISSY WALKER

ELITE HEIRS OF MANHATTAN SERIES

Seductive Hearts

Sweet Surrender

Sinful Desires

Silent Cravings

Sensual Games

ELITE MEN OF MANHATTAN SERIES

Forbidden Lust*

Forbidden Love*

Lost Love

Missing Love

Guarded Love

Infinite Love Novella

ELITE MAFIA OF NEW YORK SERIES

Cruel Lust*

Stolen Love

Finding Love

SLATER SIBLINGS SERIES

Hungry Heart

Chained Heart

Iron Heart

*Forbidden Lust/Love are a duet and to be read in order.

*Cruel Lust is a trilogy and to be read in order

All other books are stand alones.

JOIN MISSY'S BOOK BABES

Hear about exclusive book releases, teasers, discounts and book bundles before anyone else.

Sign up to Missy's newsletter here:
www.authormissywalker.com

Become part of Missy's Facebook Reader Group where we chat all things books, releases and of course fun giveaways!

https://www.facebook.com/groups/missywalkersbookbabes

ACKNOWLEDGMENTS

Big shoutout to my amazing editors, Chantell, Kay, and Nicki—your feedback seriously made all the difference. And to my awesome beta readers, Ella, Karmin, Maria, and Saskia, you guys were absolute lifesavers, helping me get this story just right.

A huge thank you to my incredible fans, especially my Facebook reader group, Missy Walker's Book Babes! Building this community has been such an amazing experience, and I love seeing everything you all share.

We all need a little escape sometimes, and that's exactly what I try to give with each book. Life's no easy street, but I hope my stories bring you some light when you need it, and that our reader family continues to support one another.

Much love,
 Missy x

ABOUT THE AUTHOR

Missy is an Australian author who writes kissing books with equal parts angst and steam. Stories about billionaires, forbidden romance, and second chances roll around in her mind probably more than they ought to.

When she's not writing, she's taking care of her two daughters and doting husband and conjuring up her next saucy plot.

Inspired by the acreage she lives on, Missy regularly distracts herself by visiting her orchard, baking naughty but delicious foods, and socialising with her girl squad.

Then there's her overweight cat—Charlie, chickens, and border collie dog—Benji if she needed another excuse to pass the time.

If you like Missy Walker's books, consider leaving a review and following her here:

instagram.com/missywalkerauthor
facebook.com/AuthorMissyWalker
tiktok.com/@authormissywalker
bookbub.com/profile/missy-walker

Printed in Great Britain
by Amazon